LACOMBE, LUCIEN

D0809587

LOUIS MALLE AND PATRICK MODIANO

LACOMBE, LUCIEN

TRANSLATED FROM THE FRENCH BY SABINE DESTRÉE

A RICHARD SEAVER BOOK / THE VIKING PRESS / NEW YORK

© Éditions Gallimard, 1974

English language translation Copyright © 1975
by The Viking Press, Inc.

All rights reserved

A *Richard Seaver Book/The Viking Press*

First published in 1975 by The Viking Press, Inc.
625 Madison Avenue, New York, N.Y. 10022

Published simultaneously in Canada by
The Macmillan Company of Canada Limited

Library of Congress Cataloging in Publication Data
Malle, Louis, 1932-
    Lacombe, Lucien: the complete scenario of the film
by Louis Malle.
"A Richard Seaver book."
    I. Modiano, Patrick, 1947-   joint author.
II. Lacombe, Lucien. [Motion picture]
PN1997.L13M3513   842′.9′14   74-7901
ISBN 0-670-00583-5

Printed in U.S.A.

Pierre Blaise, who plays Lucien, and director Louis Malle.

Producer and Director	Louis Malle
Associate Producer	Claude Nedjar
Screenplay	Louis Malle and Patrick Modiano
Director of Photography	Tonino Delli Colli
Art Director	Ghislain Uhry
Editor	Suzanne Baron
Sound	Jean-Claude Laureux
Production Supervisor	Paul Maigret

CAST

LUCIEN	Pierre Blaise
FRANCE	Aurore Clément
ALBERT HORN	Holger Lowenadler
BELLA HORN	Thérèse Gieshe
JEAN BERNARD	Stéphane Buoy
BETTY BEAULIEU	Loumi Iacobesco
FAURE	René Bouloc
AUBERT	Pierre Decazes
TONIN	Jean Rougerie
MME. LACOMBE	Gilberte Rivet
MONSIEUR LABORIT	Jacques Rispal

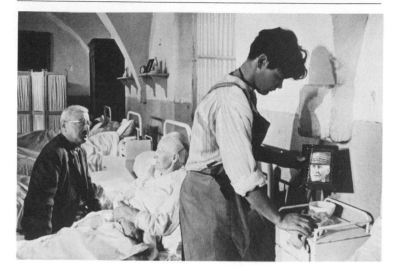

1

In a charitable nursing home for the elderly a young seventeen-year-old employee is scrubbing the floor of the women's dormitory.

Most of the beds, with perhaps a dozen exceptions, are empty. There are a few visitors, and two or three nuns who work in the nursing home. The murmur of conversations. It is afternoon of a beautiful early-summer day. The shades are drawn.

The young boy, whose name is Lucien, is clearly a good worker. As he makes his way among the beds, he opens the night tables, takes out the chamber pots, and empties them one by one into a large pail. At the far end of the room another menial worker is doing the same job; slightly older than Lucien, he works less energetically than his co-worker. On several occasions the room resounds with his laughter.

Lucien comes over to a bed occupied by an old lady who is in deep conversation with an elderly man seated close beside her. The two old people make a point of breaking off their conversation when Lucien approaches; they look at him, then exchange glances, but Lucien appears oblivious to their little games. He dusts the night table at the head of the bed, lifting up a framed picture of Marshal Pétain, across which is draped a rosary.

As she walks past, one of the nuns turns on an oversized radio hung on the wall to hear Philippe Henriot's daily afternoon chat. Lucien picks up his scrub cloth and wrings it out. He is standing next to an open window; he pauses in his rounds and leans out.

In the garden below, a number of elderly people are taking their constitutionals, moving at a snail's pace, or sunning themselves on the benches.

Lucien raises his eyes. On the branch of a tree a robin sings and hops about. Lucien takes a peasant's slingshot from his pocket, aims carefully, and lets fly. The bird falls into the courtyard below.

Lucien resumes his work. No one, in the dormitory or in the courtyard, has noticed his act. Clément, Lucien's fellow worker, comes up to him, whispers something in his ear, claps him on the back, and bursts out laughing, to the indignation of the old people and nuns who are listening to Philippe Henriot.

2

    Wearing a peasant jacket and beret, Lucien is riding a bicycle along a narrow country road. A suitcase made of reinforced cardboard is tied to the luggage rack. The sun is still low in the sky, but it promises to be another beautiful day. It is Sunday, and Lucien seems happy.

    As he approaches his village—whose name, Souleillac, is indicated by a roadsign—Lucien passes a herd of sheep. A big dog runs after him, snapping at his heels. The girl taking care of the sheep laughs and calls after him in a mocking tone: "So long, Lucien!" She calls her dog back.

Lucien, still riding his bicycle, at the outskirts of the village, turns off the road and enters the courtyard of a farm, which consists of a main building, a smaller dwelling, and several other buildings including a barn and pigeon coop. The barnyard is filled with all kinds of animals. Lucien heads directly for the smaller house, parks his bicycle, and shoves open the door.

Inside, a family—a father, mother, and five young children—is eating breakfast. Lucien seems surprised and upset.

LUCIEN: What the hell are you doing in my house?

Emile, the father, gets up with a smile. He is a short but strapping man, who walks with a limp. He extends his hand to Lucien.

ÉMILE: Are you Lucien, Thérèse's boy?

Lucien refuses to shake hands. He walks over to the table.

LUCIEN (pointing to the dishes and silverware): All that's not yours. Those are my father's plates and dishes. . . .

ÉMILE (still smiling): Maybe they are! . . . Go see the boss, he'll fill you in. . . .

Lucien stares at him, then heads toward a big armoire at the far end of the room. He brusquely pulls a chair out from under one of the children, a little boy of four, and climbs up on it, in order to reach something on top of the armoire. Hidden up there is a hunting rifle, wrapped in rags, and some shells. He climbs back down, unwraps the rags so that the gun is fully visible, and points it at Émile and his family.

LUCIEN (threateningly): Just make sure you don't cause any damage to anything here, or you'll have to answer to me. . . .

Émile is still smiling. Lucien suddenly heads for the door. As he passes Émile, the latter tosses after him, in a mocking tone:

ÉMILE: My name, in case you'd like to know, is
Émile. . . .

3

    *Still carrying the rifle, Lucien reaches the main house.
The shutters of a second-story window open, and a woman of
about forty, dressed in a long nightgown, appears in the window.
It's Thérèse, Lucien's mother. Behind her, for a brief moment,
a man in shirtsleeves appears: Laborit, the owner of the farm.
He is about sixty, but in very good shape for a man of his years.*

4

Lucien is seated at a table in the room of the main house which serves not only as kitchen and dining room but also as living area. There is a large fireplace. Thérèse, who is now dressed, puts a plate of soup, some bread, and giblets in front of Lucien, who puts down the hunting rifle he has been carefully cleaning with a cloth, and begins to eat. Lucien watches his mother, who seems ill at ease as she bustles about the room.

THÉRÈSE (*not looking at Lucien*): How come you took out your father's rifle?

Lucien doesn't answer.

THÉRÈSE: You know it's against the law. . . .

Lucien takes some money from his pocket and hands it to her.

LUCIEN: Here, I got a twenty-franc raise. . . .

Thérèse comes over to take the money, quickly counts it, and stuffs it into her apron pocket.

THÉRÈSE (*mechanically*): I'm glad to hear it. . . .

Laborit, who is still dressing, comes into the room and goes over and sits down across from Lucien.

LABORIT (*in good humor*): Morning, Lucien.

LUCIEN: Good morning, Monsieur Laborit.

Thérèse brings a plate of soup over to Laborit and sets it down in front of him.

LABORIT (*to Thérèse, without any sign of animosity*): He could at least let us know, your boy could, when he's coming to pay a visit. . . . (*To Lucien*) Are you staying for a while?

LUCIEN: I have two days off. . . .

Both men are eating heartily and diligently, as Thérèse continues to bustle about the room.

LUCIEN (*to Thérèse, aggressively*): And what about those other people? What the hell are they doing in our house?

As he is speaking, Lucien points in the general direction of the smaller dwelling.

THÉRÈSE (*not looking at him*): They're helping Monsieur Laborit. I let them have the house. . . .

LUCIEN (*looking at Laborit*): I see there're some changes around here.

LABORIT (*irritated*): The work's got to get done! With your father a prisoner, and Joseph gone off. . . .

LUCIEN: Oh? I didn't know!

LABORIT (*shrugging his shoulders*): He's gone off and joined the underground, that good-for-nothing has! (*He laughs.*) My son's a patriot, now what do you think of that!

5

A procession of fifty or so villagers dressed in their Sunday best, mostly women, follow the priest, who is carrying the Blessèd Sacrament. The priest is surrounded by several altar boys with censers. The procession moves slowly along a narrow, rocky path not far from the village. The villagers are singing a hymn to the Virgin Mary.

Somewhere in the middle of the procession Lucien is talking to a boy roughly his own age, but we cannot hear what they are saying. Laborit and Lucien's mother are directly ahead of them in the procession. His mother turns around; Lucien begins to sing with the others.

6

At night, under bright moonlight, Lucien, who is carrying a rifle, walks through a dell, followed by a younger boy who seems somewhat uneasy. The younger boy is carrying a game bag. They emerge into a kind of clearing, where, at the base of a cliff, a dozen or so rabbits are frolicking. The rabbits don't even turn and run away as the boys approach.

Lucien opens fire: two shots, one rabbit. He reloads the rifle and fires again, moving forward as he does. One feels that he is enjoying—an intense, physical enjoyment—what he is doing. He stops, out of cartridges. He lies down in the grass and rests his head against the ground as he watches the younger boy gather up the last rabbits he has shot. The boy comes back and sits down beside Lucien without saying a word. Lucien seems worn out but happy.

7

In the courtyard of the farm Lucien, his mother, and Émile's wife are seated on chopping blocks, plucking chickens. Émile's children are playing in the background.

LUCIEN: Did you find the rabbits on the table?

THÉRÈSE: Monsieur Laborit isn't happy about your hunting. The whole village heard you.

Lucien doesn't answer.

THÉRÈSE: You're just like your father!

Lucien glances at her, then gets up and starts chasing a chicken, which manages to elude his grasp several times. Lucien is clearly enjoying the game; finally he catches the chicken by literally throwing himself full-length on top of it. He gets to his feet and in the same movement wrings its neck, then gives the chicken to his mother.

LUCIEN (*suddenly*): You know, I don't want to go back to that old-people's home!

Thérèse goes on plucking her chicken. She casts a quick, somewhat embarrassed glance at Émile's wife, who is so absorbed in what she is doing that she fails to note it.

THÉRÈSE: You ought to be happy you have a job. . . .

LUCIEN: I'm not.

THÉRÈSE (*softly*): You can't stay here, Lucien. Laborit wouldn't want you here. . . . (*Pause.*) When your father comes back. . . .

LUCIEN (*interrupting*): When he comes back, there's going to be hell to pay.

Thérèse glances over at him, but does not reply.

8

Lucien, carrying a rabbit in his hand, arrives at the village square. He heads for the school, whose windows are wide open, and glances inside. A dozen or so children, varying in age from six to thirteen, are seated at their desks. The schoolmaster, a man named Peyssac, is reading aloud a text, which the older children are copying, and at the same time is keeping a watchful eye on the younger ones.

PEYSSAC (*reading*): "It was a stormy afternoon, and in the distance the thunder rumbled, a muffled avalanche. . . ."

Peyssac lifts his eyes from the page and sees Lucien.

PEYSSAC (*to Lucien*): You can come in, Lucien. . . .

Lucien goes into the classroom. Peyssac has picked up the text that one of the pupils has been writing.

PEYSSAC (*excessively*): Maurice, I'm afraid there's not much hope for you. . . . Your case is hopeless. Do you see what you did? . . . No, I don't mean the smudges on the paper from your dirty hands. I mean your spelling: you think "stormy" is written "S-T-A-U-R-M-Y"? Well (*shrugging his shoulders*), what can I say? I also have to admit one doesn't have to know how to spell to be a shepherd. (*He tosses Maurice's text back onto his desk, in a gesture of weariness.*)

Peyssac's little joke draws a predictably easy response from the other pupils, who burst out laughing.
Peyssac looks at his watch.

PEYSSAC: Time's up! You can leave, children. . . .

The children make a mad dash for the door, pushing and shoving one another as they go. Peyssac goes over to the blackboard, erases what is written on it, writes the following day's date and then a character-training sentence below it. As he is doing this, he talks to Lucien, who has walked up toward Peyssac's desk.

PEYSSAC: What do you want?

Lucien puts the rabbit on Peyssac's desk.

LUCIEN: I brought you a little present. . . .

Peyssac glances at the rabbit.

PEYSSAC (*ironically*): Thanks. Is that why you came to see me?

LUCIEN (*suddenly*): I want to join the underground.

PEYSSAC (*still writing on the blackboard*): And what does that have to do with me?

LUCIEN: Well, you're the one who says yes or no. . . . Joseph told me you were. . . .

Peyssac turns around and looks at Lucien.

PEYSSAC: First of all, you're too young. . . . And besides, we have as many people as we need.

Lucien remains silent.

PEYSSAC (*with a certain sternness*): And anyway, this is serious business. It's no lark, Lucien, like going out and poaching. . . . It's like being in the army, you know. . . .

He comes over and puts a hand on Lucien's shoulder.

PEYSSAC: Listen, wait a little while and we'll see. . . .

9

Lucien and the shepherdess he passed as he arrived by bicycle in the village the day before are seated on a little wall in a wild, rock-strewn spot not far from Souleillac, which is situated on a limestone plateau in southern France. It is another beautiful day. Around them, as they sit in silence, thirty or so sheep slowly move and graze.

Later, as the sun is going down, they gather the sheep together and lead them along a path flanked on both sides by high stone walls, on the side of a hill. Lucien stops and gazes out over the countryside below. He walks over toward the edge of the cliff and looks at the setting sun.

The girl waits for him for a moment or two, then runs after her departing sheep.

Lucien, still gazing at the sun, blinks a few times. He seems fascinated by the view. From the distance, we hear the girl's voice calling him, but Lucien doesn't seem to hear.

10

Lucien, Émile, and two neighboring farmers are dragging from the barn the enormous body of Laborit's workhorse, Boy, whose legs are already stiffened. They have a great deal of trouble getting the body through the barn door. Laborit, without actually lifting a finger to help, is directing the operation.

The men, who are speaking the local provincial dialect, are laughing and joking together. Lucien remains silent; his face is completely inscrutable, almost wooden, as he holds the horse's head. And yet he seems very affected by Boy's death.

After a lot of strenuous heave-hoing, the carcass is finally placed on a big cart, which normally is used to carry away the garbage. The men give a collective sigh of relief and congratulate one another on a job well done.

> LABORIT: He was a good horse, Boy was. Be a long time before I find another like him. . . . C'mon, let's go have a little snort. . . .

As the men head toward the house, still joking back and forth, Lucien remains behind with Boy, timidly patting his neck and withers.

11

Once again Lucien is riding his bicycle, with his suitcase tied onto the baggage rack, down a long, deserted country road. He stops, gets off, and sees that he has a flat tire. We hear him swear—a hearty "Shit!"—and then he starts off on foot, holding the handlebars.

He enters the town. It is another bright moonlit night. The street is completely empty. Lucien emerges into a small town square, where two men are busy unloading a truck very hurriedly, while a third stands guard. The guard, taken aback at seeing Lucien suddenly appear, comes over to him.

> MAN: Where did you come from?

Lucien continues on his way, still holding his bike by the handlebars. We hear the sound of marching boots. Lucien quickly takes refuge in a porte-cochere, just before a German patrol marches past. Lucien smiles, waits till the patrol is gone, then continues on his route.

Now he is walking in a broader street, on the outskirts of town, which is flanked on both sides by houses that appear to have been built at the turn of the century. Lucien hears a car coming and again hides. A black Citroën sedan drives by, slows down, and turns to drive through a gate a few yards from where Lucien is standing. Lucien takes a few steps in the direction of the gate and sees the car stop in front of the steps of a large villa that has a curiously medieval appearance. A man and two women get out of the car, laughing and jostling each other as they go up the steps and into the house.

The man has grabbed each of the girls around the waist.

Above the gate is a sign bearing the words in large letters: GROTTO HOTEL AND RESTAURANT.

There are other cars parked in the area in front of the hotel.

Next to the front entrance there is a veranda which projects beyond the line of the rest of the building. There are no curtains, the lights are on (this is the only house in the town that we have seen with lights on). We see shadows moving back and forth. Through an open window we hear peals of laughter and a phonograph playing one of André Claveau's popular songs.

A girl appears at the window and leans on the sill, till a man appears behind her, grabs her, and pulls her back into the room. She gives a shriek. Fascinated and intrigued, Lucien sets his bicycle down and moves forward till he is next to a shrub, which hides him from the view of those inside. He cranes to see what's going on beyond the veranda windows.

A man armed with a submachine gun walks up behind Lucien and, without making a sound, grabs Lucien by the neck. Lucien struggles to free himself, but the man sticks the barrel of the gun straight into Lucien's midsection. With his free hand he frisks Lucien to make sure he isn't armed, then gives him a couple of well-placed slaps across the face.

SENTINEL: So, the kid's spying, eh? Okay, you, move. We'll see what you have to say for yourself. . . .

He pushes him roughly in the direction of the hotel.

12

Lucien, still being manhandled by the sentinel who discovered him, is shoved into the lobby of the hotel, on one side

of which is a broad curving staircase. Another sentinel is slumped in an easy chair, half asleep.

Beneath the staircase an elegant couple: Betty Beaulieu, a very pretty but also very mannered girl, and Jean-Bernard de Voisins, a good-looking young man with all the affectations of a dandy.

JEAN-BERNARD (*to Betty*) : Any news from Paris?

Betty's dog, a superb Great Dane, is lying beside her. As Lucien arrives, the dog gets to its feet and begins to growl threateningly as though it were about to leap at Lucien's throat. Betty calls out to the dog.

BETTY: Kid! Come here, Kid! . . . Here Kid, here Kid!

The sentinel pushes Lucien into a neighboring room in which there are a bar and three tables. Dazzled by the light, Lucien looks around.

Behind the bar is a petite brunette, Marie, a maid and waitress, whose features to say the least are uneven. Next to her is a good-looking man in his middle thirties, Henri Aubert, whose hair is slicked down with brilliantine. Aubert is mixing drinks in a cocktail shaker as he whispers sweet nothings to a buxom blonde seated across the bar from him; from her laughter she seems to be appreciative of his remarks. All around the bar are numerous photographs showing Aubert in the pose of a bicycle racer.

Through a door on one side is visible a large dining room in which a dozen or so people are having dinner. A few couples are dancing in the area between the tables.

Seated at a table in the bar itself is Tonin, a portly man of about fifty with the bloated face of an alcoholic. He is playing cards with two German noncommissioned officers.

At another table in the bar two women, who seem strangely calm in the midst of all the uproar, are talking. One is Lucienne, Tonin's companion, who is very prim and proper; the other is Madame Georges, a mysterious character with very masculine traits.

Lucien, dumfounded by the surroundings and the events of the previous few minutes, stands stock still in the middle of the room. The murmur of conversation ceases. All eyes turn toward him.

TONIN: Who is he?

THE SENTINEL: I found him out in the garden. . . . He was spying on the place.

LUCIEN: No I wasn't. . . . I wasn't doing anything. I was on my way back to the nursing home. . . .

Aubert comes over to him.

AUBERT: Listen, kid, don't you know there's a curfew? Don't you know you're not supposed to be out in the streets after ten o'clock?

Lucien stares back at him fixedly, without replying.

AUBERT: What's wrong with you, kid? What're you looking at me like that for?

LUCIEN: Aren't you Henri Aubert, the bicycle racer?

AUBERT (*with a vain smile*): You seen me race, kid?

LUCIEN (*admiringly*): Yes. In 'thirty-nine, with my father. For the Caussade Grand Prix.

AUBERT (*smiling*): I remember. . . . Where you from, the town?

LUCIEN: No. From Souleillac. . . .

AUBERT: Uh-huh. . . . I know some people from Souleillac. The lady who runs the grocery store, what's her name again?

LUCIEN: Madame Cabessut.

AUBERT (*smiling*): That's it, Madame Cabessut. Dark hair. . . .

Lucienne gets to her feet and goes over to whisper something in Tonin's ear. Tonin in turn rises, his eyes fixed on Lucien. Then, with the broad gesture of a drunkard, he puts an arm around Lucien's shoulder and leads him toward the bar.

TONIN: Come on, let's have a drink.

They reach the bar, with Tonin's arm still draped affectionately around Lucien's shoulders. Lucienne has followed them.

TONIN: Marie, two Suzes. (*To Lucien*) So, you're from Souleillac, eh?

LUCIEN: You ever been there?

TONIN (*placing a glass in Lucien's hand and clinking glasses with him*): Beautiful country, really beautiful. Wild country. . . . But like you say, that's limestone country. . . . The area's filled with Resistance people, or so they say. Is that what you heard?

Lucien gulps down part of his glass. He smiles.

LUCIEN: Oh, you don't see much of them, you know.

Aubert, playing Tonin's game, joins in.

AUBERT: How is Madame Cabessut anyway? Still in the pink of health? . . . Here, have another drink. . . .

Later. *The lights are all out, except for a fat lamp on the bar. Lucien is leaning on the bar, a glass in one hand. He is drunk. He is literally surrounded by Tonin, Lucienne, and Aubert, and seems flattered to be the object of so much attention.*

LUCIENNE: And what's the name of this schoolteacher?

LUCIEN: Peyssac. . . . Peyssac, Robert. They say he's a Freemason. . . . Say, what's a Freemason anyway?

TONIN: And he's the one who's in charge? Are you sure?

LUCIEN (*decisively*): Yeah, I'm sure. . . . Only under another name. . . .

TONIN: What name?

LUCIEN: Wait a minute. . . . I have it: Voltaire, that's what they call him. Lieutenant Voltaire.

Lucien obviously doesn't feel well. He finishes his drink and tries to climb up on a bar stool.

LUCIEN: Can I sit down?

13

Lucien, *still fully dressed, is asleep on a couch.*

The room, which now serves as Tonin's office, used to be the main lobby of the hotel. The door to the room opens onto the hallway and the stairway. The lobby furniture is still intact, but to it has been added a long wooden table on which are a typewriter and several files. On one wall a map of the area. Numerous files are strewn throughout the room.

The door half opens. Marie comes in and walks over to the couch.

MARIE (*shaking Lucien*): Wake up! Come on, it's time to wake up!

LUCIEN (*turning over; he has trouble opening his eyes*): What?

MARIE: It's time to wake up! Mademoiselle Chauvelot will be here any minute!

Lucien pulls himself up and sits on the edge of the couch, holding his forehead in his hands.

LUCIEN: My head! Oh, my head!

MARIE (*with compassion*): Poor boy. . . . You drank too much last night. . . . Want some coffee? And how about some aspirin?

She runs her fingers through his hair.

LUCIEN: Yeah. . . .

Marie leaves the room. Lucien yawns, gets up, and walks to the window. Lucienne comes in. She is dressed very primly and has her hair done up in a chignon. Under her arm she is carrying a file. She sits down immediately at her desk and places the file in front of her.

LUCIENNE (*looking at Lucien*): Good morning, young man. . . .

LUCIEN (*intimidated*): Good morning, Madame.

LUCIENNE (*stiffening*): Mademoiselle!

Marie returns, bearing a platter on which are a bowl of steaming café au lait, some bread and butter.

MARIE (*to Lucienne*): I'm sorry, Mademoiselle Chauvelot, but we didn't have a room for him. . . .

LUCIENNE: Don't worry. That's all right.

Lucien, his mouth full of food, nods at her. Lucienne opens her file, riffles through the contents, stamping them as she goes. Lucien, still munching his breakfast, watches her.

A young German soldier, a sergeant major, comes into the room and goes straight to Lucienne's desk. He shakes hands with her and she responds with a broad smile.

SOLDIER (*amiably*): Good morning, Fräulein Chauvelot.

LUCIENNE: And how are you this morning?

SOLDIER: Fine, thank you.

LUCIENNE: Just a second, I'm almost finished. . . .

SOLDIER: What a beautiful day. . . .

LUCIENNE: What you mean is: another scorcher!

She stamps a few more sheets of paper, closes the file, and shakes hands with the soldier.

LUCIENNE: This is for Monsieur Müller. . . .

SOLDIER (*taking the file*): *Einverstanden,* Fräulein Chauvelot. . . . *Auf Wiedersehen.* . . .

He shakes hands with her and leaves.

Lucien has been observing the scene with an amazed expression.

Lucienne takes from the table a tall pile of envelopes and begins to sort them.

LUCIENNE: They are most obliging. . . . And punctual. . . . If we had been like them, we would have won the war. . . . Oh, damn! I just broke one of my fingernails! (*She looks at her forefinger.*)

Tonin comes in, in a state of disarray, followed by a young barber, who is carrying the tools of his trade.

TONIN (*to Lucienne*): What were you just saying, Mama?

LUCIENNE: I just broke a fingernail.

Tonin goes over and kisses her on the forehead.

LUCIENNE (*reprovingly*): You've been drinking, Pierre. It's bad for you in the morning. . . .

TONIN (*playing the child*): Only one little Suze, Mama. It's good for you. My morning pick-me-up. With all this heat, you'd think you were in Indochina. . . .

He sits down on a chair in the middle of the room. The young man drapes a towel around his shoulders and begins to cut his hair.

TONIN (*to Lucien*): How are you this morning, young fellow?

LUCIEN: Okay, Monsieur Tonin.

TONIN (*to Lucienne, as he points to Lucien*): Don't you find he looks like Paul?

LUCIENNE (*slowly shaking her head*): Yes, maybe. . . . Paul was thinner. . . .

TONIN: How about reading me the morning mail, Mama. . . .

Lucienne takes a letter at random from the pile and begins to read.

LUCIENNE: "Gentlemen of the Gestapo: As a farm worker and recipient of my country's military medal, I write you to inform you of the dubious undertakings of one Louvel, Étienne. Not only has the person named above. . . .

As she is reading we hear the sound of voices in the entrance hallway. Lucienne breaks off reading when Peyssac, the school-teacher, is shoved into the room—handcuffed—by Henri Aubert, who is wearing a coat, and by another member of the group named Faure, a weasel-faced man of about thirty who looks like an intellectual and has an ingratiating air.

> AUBERT (jovially, to Tonin): Here, we're delivering you a certain Lieutenant Voltaire. On a silver platter. . . . We found him in bed. He was sleeping like an angel. . . .

> FAURE: We also found some tracts on his night table, the poor innocent fellow. . . . (He reads from one of the tracts.) "The German troops are retreating on all fronts. Soon you will be free, in a Free France. . . ." They at least ought to have the courtesy to take a fair poll. . . . Me, for instance: I don't want to be freed by the Rothschild Bank. . . . That's my privilege, right?

Lucien, obviously taken aback, stares at Peyssac, who is holding his head high. Lucien walks over to Peyssac.

> LUCIEN (very close, in a near whisper): Monsieur Peyssac, what. . . .

> PEYSSAC (softly): Shut up, you bastard!

The young barber sprinkles some hair oil on Tonin's hair.

> TONIN: Welcome, Monsieur Peyssac. We wish you a very pleasant stay. (To Faure) Take him upstairs. I'll be right up. . . .

> FAURE: Do you want me to start in?

> TONIN (irritated): No. Wait till I get there. . . .

Faure shrugs his shoulders and shoves Peyssac toward the door.

FAURE: Funny, but for some reason I never liked school teachers.

AUBERT (*to Tonin*): All right. If you don't need me any longer, I'm going to take a shower.

Aubert in turn leaves the room.

FAURE (*voice over*): I don't know why. They're all socialists, every last one of them. What about you: are you a socialist?

Lucien goes over to Tonin.

LUCIEN: What are you going to do with him?

The barber adds some brilliantine to Tonin's hair and carefully begins to comb it.

TONIN: We're going to have a little talk. . . . (*He smiles.*) Don't worry! (*To Lucienne*) We'll have to think up something to keep this young man busy. . . .

LUCIENNE (*with great authority*): He can start by opening my mail for me.

Lucien goes over to where Lucienne is sitting. She hands him a pile of letters and a knife.

LUCIENNE (*opening a letter with a knife*): Here, that's the way you do it.

Lucien follows suit, but in contrast to her efforts, his are awkward and clumsy.

TONIN: Go on, Mama, read some more. . . .

LUCIENNE (*opening a letter, and reading it mechanically*): "I feel obliged to draw your attention to Madame Leboeuf, Solange, who runs a millinery shop in the town of Lubsac. Her two sons, who are rebels and Communists, pay her frequent visits. Why, only yesterday. . . ."

TONIN (*bored*): That's enough, that's enough. . . .

Lucienne takes another letter that Lucien hands to her.

LUCIENNE: "As a practicing Catholic, and as someone who as a Frenchman and Christian finds the black market reprehensible. . . ."

TONIN (*raising his arm to stop her*): Is that all there is? Nothing of any consequence in the morning mail?

LUCIENNE (*selecting a piece of paper*): Yes, one matter. The Préfecture is lodging a complaint against the disappearance of Doctor Pradines.

TONIN: Don't let it bother you, Mama. . . . It'll be a cold day in hell before they find their Doctor Pradines. . . .

The barber holds up a mirror at various angles so that Tonin can see his neck and temples. Tonin nods approval, gets to his feet, and yawns.

TONIN: Okay. Time to take care of Voltaire.

He laughs and exits quickly from the room. The young barber folds up his towels, puts away his scissors, and also leaves.

Meanwhile, Lucien goes on opening the mail, handing the letters to Lucienne, who sorts them into their various files.

LUCIEN (*haltingly*): Are you . . . are you Monsieur Tonin's mother?

LUCIENNE (*shrugging her shoulders*): Don't be silly! Of course not. . . .

She opens a drawer, takes out another bundle of letters, and places them on the table in front of Lucien.

LUCIEN: There are a lot more where they came from?

LUCIENNE (*her eyes still lowered*): We receive approximately two hundred a day. There was even one gentleman who wrote us informing against himself . . . accusing himself of crimes against the State. (*She shrugs her shoulders.*) It's like a sickness. . . .

Lucien goes on opening the letters.

LUCIENNE (*reading, and underlining something in red as she does*): What about you? . . . You want to work for the police? Be part of them?

LUCIEN: I don't know.

LUCIENNE: You're young. . . . (*She looks at him.*) I have a feeling that Inspector Lanciaga likes you a lot.

LUCIEN (*surprised*): You mean Monsieur Tonin's an inspector?

Lucienne puts down her pencil. She has a faraway look in her eyes.

LUCIENNE (*speaking more to herself than to Lucien*): He was . . . an extraordinary policeman. . . .

LUCIEN (*hesitantly*): And . . . he isn't any more?

She looks at him.

LUCIENNE (*with feeling*): They fired him, in 'thirty-six, as unsuitable! . . .

14

Later. Lucien is walking from the office to a hallway. His clogs make a loud noise on the tile floor. From the second floor we hear a shout, a loud scream of pain. Lucien walks over to the stairway, his eyes raised. Two children of five or six are running downstairs, chasing each other. We hear another scream. Marie appears through a small door beneath the stairway, carrying a tray of glasses.

MARIE: You can't play there, children! Run along now!

She smiles at Lucien and goes into the bar. Lucien hears the click of a ping-pong ball and peals of laughter. He heads for the door beneath the staircase.

He emerges into a large room in considerable disorder; there is no furniture and in one corner a number of packing cases are piled every which way. In the middle of the room Betty Beaulieu and Jean-Bernard de Voisins are playing ping-pong. Betty, who is wearing a skirt with matching shorts beneath and a kerchief in her hair, punctuates her playing with strident little-girl screams. Lucien walks over to them and stands there watching them for a moment. They are talking as they play.

BETTY (*to Jean-Bernard*): Tell me, Jean, baby. . . .

JEAN-BERNARD: What, darling?

BETTY: There just *has* to be a gypsy nightclub in Toulouse, now doesn't there?

JEAN-BERNARD (*wearily*): No, darling. In Toulouse there's nothing. Not a damn thing!

BETTY: Then when will you take me to Spain? You promised you'd take me soon to San Sebastián.

JEAN-BERNARD: I will, darling, I promise.

Meanwhile, Lucien has gone over to where Henri Aubert, a towel around his neck and his hair still wet from his shower, is busily cleaning a number of pistols laid out on a table in front of him. Behind him, on a gun rack, there are several submachine guns. Aubert looks up at Lucien and smiles.

AUBERT: You ever fire one of these things?

LUCIEN: No.

AUBERT: Nothing simpler.

He places a Luger in Lucien's hand and shows him the correct arm position.

AUBERT (*technically*): Relax, you have to keep it free and easy. . . .

Aubert points to the far wall, a few yards away, on which is pasted a large poster of Marshal Pétain, under which is written in big letters: "Are You More French Than He?"

AUBERT: Aim at the left nostril.

Lucien takes careful aim and fires. Betty, who is still playing ping-pong in the background, gives another high-pitched scream.

AUBERT: I told you to aim at the left nostril, not the cap!

Lucien fires again.

AUBERT: That's better. But you're still lifting your arm too much. . . . You're too stiff!

He corrects Lucien's position, and once again he aims and fires. Meanwhile, in the background, Betty and Jean-Bernard are fighting. Betty taps her foot in irritation.

BETTY: What in the world's come over you, anyway! What right do you have to talk to me in that way! (*She tosses her paddle down.*) And besides, I'm fed up with

ÉTES-VOUS PLUS FRANÇAIS QUE LUI ?

this damn grease spot in the road. I'm going back to Paris!

JEAN-BERNARD: You knew very well that we can't, darling.

BETTY: Just because you happened to write some checks that bounced is no reason for me to stay here and rot. I'm fed up. *Fed up!* I have to go back to Paris. I have to see Greven and sign my contract with Continental Films! . . . Do you hear me?

And she stalks out of the room.

Jean-Bernard wipes his forehead in a gesture of weariness. He comes over to where Lucien is shooting and watches him.

> AUBERT (*to Jean-Bernard*): He's a better shot than you are. . . .

> JEAN-BERNARD: That's not saying much! . . . (*To Lucien*) Are you staying on with us?

> LUCIEN: I don't know.

He keeps on firing, clearly with great concentration.

15

Jean-Bernard and Lucien appear in the parking lot in front of the hotel and climb into a high-powered Delahaye sports car. While Jean-Bernard, behind the wheel, slips on some very elegant half-leather, half-cotton gloves and revs up the motor, Lucien caresses the dashboard, then opens the glove compartment, discovers a pair of sunglasses, and puts them on. (He will keep on wearing them, even when they visit Horn.)

LUCIEN: Where we going?

JEAN-BERNARD: To Albert Horn's. (*Looking at Lucien, with a smile*) You mean to say you never heard of him? . . . Why, he's one of the best tailors in Paris!

With those words, the Delahaye starts off and disappears into the distance.

We see the car being driven too fast for the narrow road of the small town. It pulls up in front of a massive stone house and stops. Jean-Bernard and Lucien get out, and climb a flight of stone stairs badly in need of repair.

LUCIEN (*surprised*): He lives here?

JEAN-BERNARD: Yes. He's in hiding. (*Laughing*) He works exclusively for me. I never dreamed I'd find him here in this lousy hole. . . .

They cross a tiny garden. An elderly lady who is watering the flowers stops to watch them as they go.

JEAN-BERNARD (*obviously in the midst of a conversation*): . . . Yes, and then I was in a boarding school not far from here. At Sorèze. Ever been there?

LUCIEN: No.

JEAN-BERNARD: They threw me out. . . .

They begin to climb up a narrow spiral staircase. Jean-Bernard is whistling an André Claveau tune, "Marjolaine." He stops before a door and rings.

The door opens. Horn, a tall, distinguished-looking man about fifty, opens the door a few inches, just enough to allow his head to peek through the opening.

HORN (*to Jean-Bernard*): Oh, it's you. . . .

Jean-Bernard and Lucien follow Horn into a room remarkable for its untidiness: it is filled with furniture and old newspapers. The woodwork is lovely, but one has the feeling that the room has been unoccupied for a long time. Opposite the front door is a fairly wide hallway leading to a closed door. Against one wall of the hallway can be seen a decrepit two-burner stove and a sink. A double door opens into a large dark room, which is also cluttered with furniture draped with protective covers.

Horn closes the front door and comes over to Jean-Bernard. He is wearing a silk dressing gown and gives an overall impression of someone who has become slovenly in his ways and dress.

JEAN-BERNARD (*overly polite*): Am I intruding?

HORN (*coldly*): Not at all.

JEAN-BERNARD (*nodding to Lucien*): I've brought you a customer.

Horn scrutinizes Lucien and nods briefly in acknowledgment. Jean-Bernard slumps into a kind of broken-down couch. Lucien and Horn remain standing.

JEAN-BERNARD: It's his first suit. . . . That's an event of no small significance in the life of any man. . . .

Lucien is firmly fixed on his feet, and takes a step or two with a rolling gait.

JEAN-BERNARD: Do you remember the first visit I paid to you? My father brought me. . . . I was twelve. . . .

HORN (*with bowed head*): Yes.

Jean-Bernard lights a cigarette.

> JEAN-BERNARD: You were on the rue Marbeuf in those days. . . .

Horn seems not to have heard, and is looking Lucien up and down as though mentally taking his measurements. He points to the remnants of two bolts of cloth that are lying on a table next to the couch.

> HORN (*wearily*): Which material would the young man prefer, the Scotch plaid or the blue flannel, like the one I made you a suit from two weeks ago?

> JEAN-BERNARD: The plaid! You would prefer the plaid, wouldn't you, Lucien?

> LUCIEN (*intimidated*): Doesn't matter to me.

Horn takes his measuring tape, a pencil, and a piece of paper from the table. He begins taking Lucien's measurements.

Just then a door at the end of the hallway opens: an old lady comes into the room, carrying a cup. She appears to ignore completely the presence of Jean-Bernard and Lucien, and walks directly to Horn, who says a few words to her in German. Jean-Bernard gets to his feet and bows deferentially to her, with almost exaggerated good breeding.

JEAN-BERNARD: Madame. . . .

The old lady fails to acknowledge his greeting.

From behind his sunglasses Lucien is watching her. Still not having uttered a word, she turns and goes back to the hallway, where she takes a saucepan and starts to heat something in it. Jean-Bernard, with a worried look on his face, sits down again on the couch.

JEAN-BERNARD (*softly*): She's a strange one, your mother. . . .

Horn goes on taking Lucien's measurements, as Jean-Bernard fingers the material on the table.

JEAN-BERNARD (*musing*): These are beautiful materials. . . . I got them for a song too. . . . A few gas coupons.

. . . (*To Horn*) Did I ever tell you where they came from? From Cassels. . . . They liquidated his entire stock. Cassels was English, you know. . . .

Horn raises his eyes.

HORN: What ever happened to Cassels?

JEAN-BERNARD (*venomously*): I believe he's in some camp or other. The one at Saint-Denis, I suspect, which is reserved for the English. The Jews are at Drancy.

HORN: I know.

He has finished taking Lucien's measurements.

HORN (*to Lucien*): Thank you.

Lucien goes over and sits down on the couch next to Jean-Bernard. He plays with Jean-Bernard's lighter, then lights a cigarette.

HORN (*turning to Jean-Bernard, coldly*): The suit will be ready in five days.

JEAN-BERNARD: By the way, I have some new information about getting you to Spain. But it's going to cost you a pretty penny. . . .

HORN (*softly*): Don't you think I've already paid enough?

JEAN-BERNARD: They're going to be clamping down more and more on people like you.

HORN: Isn't the money I've already given you enough?

JEAN-BERNARD: That money, my dear fellow, was for the false papers. (*Turning to Lucien and pointing to Horn*) This gentleman is a Jew . . . a rich, miserly Jew. . . .

Suddenly we hear the sound of a piano being played in the next room. Horn goes into the other room. While we can't see him, we hear a whispered conversation that seems to be an argument. The sound of the piano ceases. Horn comes back, shutting the door between the two rooms, and says something—a sen-

tence or two—to his mother, who is moving back and forth in the hallway.

Jean-Bernard gets to his feet and goes over to Horn.

JEAN-BERNARD (*artfully*): I'll bet you miss Paris, don't you? Do you know that there are twice as many night-clubs in Paris now as there were in 'thirty-nine? So you see, war has its good sides too.

As Jean-Bernard is talking, Lucien is still playing with the cigarette lighter.

16

In the bar of the Grotto Hotel, Faure has his ear glued to the radio, listening to the Vichy government's news broadcast on the latest developments on the Normandy front. The pro-German broadcast is all one-sided and optimistic, detailing the enormous losses on the Allied side.

On the other side of the bar, Aubert and Madame Georges are discussing something in an undertone, constantly referring to some file or piece of paper in front of them. Marie comes in, carrying a tray of glasses; she passes Aubert and Madame Georges, and goes over to a table at which Lucien, Betty, Jean-Bernard, and the Great Dane are sitting. She sets down the tray. Betty takes one of the glasses and sips the contents.

BETTY (*making a wry face*): That's not a *real* pink lady!

JEAN-BERNARD: Please, darling! The young lady's doing the best she can under the circumstances.

And he winks at Marie.

BETTY: Do you know where I had the best pink lady ever? At Rudy Hiden's bar on the rue Magellan. . . . It's the best English bar in Paris. . . . (*Louder, to Faure*) How about switching to some music?

Faure turns around to her.

FAURE (*irritated*): Please, young lady! These are perilous times we're living through!

Betty makes a gesture of impatience, then turns to Lucien.

BETTY (*exuding charm*): Are you aware, Lucien, that I'm a movie actress?

LUCIEN: No. No one told me.

BETTY: Last year I had a very fine part in a film called *Night Raid*, starring Yvon Nevers. . . .

LUCIEN: You mean, people can see you in the movies?

BETTY: In Paris you could, Lucien. (*Casting a meaningful glance at Jean-Bernard*) Unfortunately, in this hellhole, the movie theaters only show old films. . . .

JEAN-BERNARD: Well, that's the way it is, I'm afraid. . . .

Jean-Bernard has gotten up and gone over to where Faure is

still listening to the radio. The news is just ending. Faure turns to Jean-Bernard with a broad smile.

FAURE: It's just as I figured. The Americans can't fight! From what I hear, they put their negroes in the front lines. . . .

JEAN-BERNARD (*ironically*): You're prejudiced, my friend. What makes you think there's any truth to the news you've just been listening to?

FAURE (*smiling*): Are you joking?

JEAN-BERNARD: Not in the least. You ought to listen to the BBC, too. That way you can take an average. Balance one against the other. . . .

Jean-Bernard starts to hunt for the BBC. Faure is sweating like a pig.

JEAN-BERNARD: Aren't you hot in your suit jacket?

FAURE: No.

Betty, who has taken from her purse one of those standard movie-actress publicity photos, is just completing her dedication to Lucien.

BETTY: There you are, Lucien! . . . (*Reading the dedication*) "To Lucien, on a night in June, with all best wishes for happiness, poetry, and success."

She hands the photo to him.

Jean-Bernard has found an English station, over which the news of the same front is, of course, quite different.

Faure, slightly in the background, is seen unfolding a newspaper, the name of which is Je Suis Partout (I Am Everywhere).

JEAN-BERNARD (*leaning over toward Faure*): Do you understand English, Stephen?

FAURE (*without taking his eyes off his newspaper*): No. What would I want to know English for?

Finally he looks up and studies Jean-Bernard evenly.

>FAURE (*in a loud voice*): I have no intention of becoming a traitor. . . . Do you want to know my honest opinion of the English? . . . They disgust me. . . .

Betty, who has caught Faure's last words, turns to him.

>BETTY (*also in a loud voice*): In any case, the English are far handsomer than the French. . . . (*To Lucien*) I was *madly* in love with Leslie Howard! . . .

Lucien appears never to have heard of Leslie Howard. He is following the discussion with interest, as though he were at the theater.

Faure turns to Jean-Bernard.

>FAURE (*smiling*): I find that even stupidity has its limits, don't you agree?

Betty, beside herself with anger, gets to her feet.

>BETTY: What was that you just said? I dare you to repeat what you just said!

Tonin, coming from the direction of the stairway, enters the room.

>TONIN (*to Betty*): You two fighting again?

He goes over to the bar.

>TONIN (*to Aubert*): Henri, give me a cognac. What are you up to? Still buying and selling like crazy?

>AUBERT: Business is business, after all.

>TONIN (*turning to Jean-Bernard and Faure*): Speaking of business, there's some waiting for both of you upstairs.

Jean-Bernard turns off the radio.

>JEAN-BERNARD: Okay. Let's get going.

>BETTY: I'm coming, too.

JEAN-BERNARD: There's no point in your coming, darling.

Tonin downs his cognac in one gulp.

TONIN: Why not, if she gets a kick out of it? . . .

Betty plants herself squarely in front of Jean-Bernard.

BETTY (*with emphasis*): Yes, it will indeed amuse me!

She leaves first, followed by Jean-Bernard and Faure. The Great Dane, lingering behind in the bar, goes over to Lucien, growling, then follows the others out.

Lucien, still seated at the same table, yawns. We hear Betty's voice drifting back as the trio starts upstairs.

BETTY (*voice over*): Personally, I don't give a damn who wins the war, the English or the Germans! . . . All I know is that I'm wasting my time here. . . . And what about my career? . . . Do you ever give my career a second's thought?

Meanwhile, Aubert is on the telephone next to the bar. Next to him, Madame Georges is consulting a notebook.

AUBERT: Hello. Reoyo? This is Henri. . . . Yes . . . yes.

MADAME GEORGES (*worried*): What's he saying? Tell me what he's saying!

AUBERT (*putting his hand over the receiver*): There are two carloads of shoes at the Spanish border. . . .

MADAME GEORGES: Carloads of shoes? And the papers to get them through?

AUBERT: He can get the papers through Guy Max, in exchange for the tungsten.

MADAME GEORGES: Tell him it's a deal.

AUBERT (*into the phone*): Reoyo. Can you hear me? It's a deal. All right. It's a deal on those terms. Fine. . . . Fine. . . .

Marie, untying her apron, leaves the bar and goes over to where Lucien is sitting.

MARIE: Do you want a cup of tea?

Lucien looks up at her and shakes his head. Marie bends over him.

MARIE (*softly*): I trust you don't intend to spend another night on the couch in Mademoiselle Chauvelot's office?

Lucien gazes at her.

MARIE: I'm going upstairs now. . . . Wait for a few minutes. . . . Mine is the fifth door on the right, at the end of the hallway.

Lucien nods assent. Marie leaves the bar.

Madame Georges and Aubert are still discussing their business affairs at the bar.

AUBERT: Did you talk to Wiroth?

MADAME GEORGES: Yes. He's going to give me a rebate on the chamois leather.

AUBERT: The krauts are really interested in that stuff?

MADAME GEORGES: In chamois leather? You have no idea. . . .

AUBERT (*admiringly*): Madame Georges, you're a truly extraordinary businesswoman. . . . And what about tanned leather?

MADAME GEORGES (*with great regret*): All they have left is untanned leather. At a very reasonable price, though. . . .

AUBERT: Very reasonable?

Lucien gets up, walks from the bar into the entranceway, almost on tiptoes.

17

Lucien reaches the second-story landing, which is completely dark. At the top of the stairs a door is ajar, emitting a thin stream of light. We can hear moans and groans, but they seem very weak. Lucien goes over to the crack in the door and, with one eye, peers inside.

What he sees is a very large bathroom, with a bathtub and double sink. To the usual accoutrements of a bathroom have been added a table, on which a typewriter perches, and a couch. Lucienne is seated at the table with the typewriter in front of her.

Faure is pacing back and forth across the room. Betty is seated on the couch.

Jean-Bernard, whose shirtsleeves are rolled up, is holding the head of some prisoner under water, for the bathtub has been filled nearly to the top. The prisoner, whose hands are handcuffed together behind his back, is struggling vainly to raise his head from the water, and in his struggle he splashes some water on Jean-Bernard, who jumps back.

Betty bursts out laughing.

BETTY: Look out for your trousers, Jean, baby!

Jean-Bernard pulls the man's head back by the hair, revealing his face: it is Peyssac, who is noisily trying to catch his breath. Just as he does, Jean-Bernard pushes his head down and shoves it back under water.

Motionless behind the door, Lucien takes in the whole scene.

Again we hear Betty's laughter, the sound of thrashing water, and then Faure's voice.

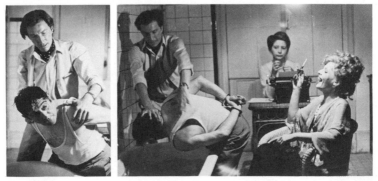

FAURE (*voice over*): Are you going to talk, you son-of-a-bitch? I swear, the way he's acting he must love this little game!

Lucien, staring fixedly in front of him, walks down the hallway. He passes Betty's Great Dane, who seems bored and accompanies him to the door of Marie's room. Lucien goes into her room. It is a tiny room, and the sole furniture is a narrow bed.

Marie is seated on the bed, letting down her hair. She gets up and puts her arms around Lucien's neck. Lucien frees himself and goes over and sits down heavily on the bed.

He sits there, lost in thought for a few seconds. Beyond the door we can still hear, more faintly, Betty's strident laughter. Marie, somewhat confused and put out, is standing in front of him, running her fingers through his hair.

MARIE: You shouldn't get involved with those people. They're not like us. . . .

She gives him a sudden shove back onto the bed.

MARIE: And anyway, it's the Americans who are going to win the war. . . . Everyone's saying it. . . .

She lies down on top of him, and kisses him.

MARIE: Did you hear what I said? (*She laughs.*) The krauts are finished. Washed up! It's the Americans, I tell you. . . .

18

Jean-Bernard and Lucien enter the garden of an impressive home on the outskirts of a small village. The garden strikes one as an oasis somehow preserved from the rigors of the war: lounging chairs, garden tables, parasols. Several children are playing, under the watchful eye of two women in summer dresses. In the background two girls are playing badminton.

Jean-Bernard and Lucien are disguised as members of the underground. Jean-Bernard is limping and holding his thigh as though he were wounded. Lucien is helping him to walk.

JEAN-BERNARD: Let me do the talking. I'm used to handling such situations. . . .

They move toward where the inhabitants of the house are sitting or playing.

JEAN-BERNARD (*under his breath*): Actually, I would have enjoyed being an actor. . . . (*He smiles.*) I think I would have been better at it than Betty. . . .

Jean-Bernard's smile again is transformed into an expression of extreme pain. A patrician-looking man in shirtsleeves, wearing a straw hat, walks toward them.

JEAN-BERNARD: Professor Vaugeois?

VAUGEOIS (*dryly*): Speaking.

JEAN-BERNARD: I'm from the Lorsac underground. The krauts attacked us a little while ago. . . . I got a bullet in the thigh. . . .

Vaugeois seems to be unsure as to what his proper conduct ought to be. He quickly looks at the two men, obviously trying to size them up.

VAUGEOIS: I'm on vacation. . . . And besides, I have nothing here to take proper care of you. . . . (*Pause.*) All right, come inside!

Vaugeois leads Jean-Bernard and Lucien into a large living room, which gives the impression—from the furniture and bric-a-brac —of having been lived in by the same family for several generations.

Lucien gazes around in amazement: this is the first time he has been in direct contact with bourgeois wealth. At the far end of the room a boy of about eighteen is putting the finishing touches to a very complicated model of an ocean liner.

VAUGEOIS (*to Jean-Bernard*): That's my son. Patrick, go and fetch my medical bag. And some alcohol.

VAUGEOIS'S SON: Yes, Father.

He hurries out of the room.

VAUGEOIS (*to Jean-Bernard*): Get off your feet. You can stretch out on the couch.

Jean-Bernard does as the doctor bids. Vaugeois begins to take off the temporary bandage. As he does, Jean-Bernard gives a moan.

JEAN-BERNARD: Some of our buddies told me about you. . . . Commander Mery especially. . . .

VAUGEOIS (*smiling*): Oh? You know Mery?

JEAN-BERNARD: Very well. . . .

VAUGEOIS (*at ease now, sure he is dealing with friends*): Mery's a friend of mine. . . . Once in a while he sends me one of his men. . . .

Vaugeois finishes unwinding the temporary bandage, sees that there is no wound, and lifts his head quizzically toward Jean-Bernard, who nonchalantly takes a Luger from his pocket and points it at the doctor.

JEAN-BERNARD (*politely*): I'm terribly sorry. German police! Sorry. . . .

He gets up and nods at Lucien.

JEAN-BERNARD: Keep him covered.

Lucien in turn takes a pistol from his pocket and points it at Vaugeois. He makes the doctor put his hands up and face the wall. Jean-Bernard goes to the window, opens it, and fires two shots in the air.

The doctor's son comes back into the room, his arms filled with bottles and bandages, followed by two women, one of whom is wearing a tennis dress.

WOMAN IN TENNIS DRESS (*terrified*): What is it, Paul? What's going on?

VAUGEOIS (*with great dignity, his hands still in the air*):
Don't be alarmed, darling.

Jean-Bernard comes back to the middle of the room and greets
the ladies. His eye catches sight of a cameo on the mantelpiece,
and he takes it.

JEAN-BERNARD (*obviously knowing whereof he speaks*):
Exquisite . . . really exquisite. . . .

He puts the cameo in his pocket. Then he walks over to where
the women are standing, as though something were bothering
him.

JEAN-BERNARD: Tell me . . . are you any relation to
Philippe Vaugeois?

The woman in the tennis dress shakes her head fearfully. Jean-
Bernard smiles.

JEAN-BERNARD: I knew him at La Baule. . . . Let's see
. . . that must have been in 'thirty-eight. Yes, Septem-
ber of 'thirty-eight. . . . First-class tennis player, Philippe. . . .

We hear the sound of cars pulling up and stopping in front of
the house.
    During this time, Lucien has been wandering through the
living room, examining the furniture, the bric-a-brac, the paint-
ings. He passes the doctor's son, who is still standing there, terrified, his arms still full of the bandages and bottles. Lucien
points with his pistol to a nineteenth-century painting depicting
a stern-countenanced lady.

LUCIEN: Who's she?

VAUGEOIS'S SON: My great-grandmother.

Lucien pauses in front of a comfortable easy chair upholstered in
English leather. He feels the padding, then sits down in the
chair, very stiffly and seriously, as though he wanted to test the
solidity of the chair. He gets up, then sits down again, more

comfortably this time, stretching out his legs. Vaugeois's son, standing stock still, follows Lucien's movements with his eyes.

Tonin, Faure, and Hippolyte (a collaborator from Martinique) come into the room.

Jean-Bernard goes over to Tonin.

JEAN-BERNARD (*pointing to Vaugeois*): It's just as we thought. The doctor works with Mery!

The two women are huddled in one corner of the room, still terrified.

MADAME VAUGEOIS (*beside herself with fear*): But do something, Paul! Call the Prefect!

VAUGEOIS: Don't worry. Everything's going to be all right.

On a table near where they are standing a telephone rings. Madame Vaugeois moves to answer it, but Hippolyte steps in. He picks up the receiver.

HIPPOLYTE (*politely*): Hello. Yes. You'd like to talk with Professor Vaugeois. . . . One moment, please. (*He turns to Tonin.*) It's the professor's brother. What shall I tell him, boss?

Tonin is in the process of examining, with professional judgment, the array of bottles containing various alcoholic beverages that are standing on a tray.

TONIN: Simply tell him that we're going to shoot his brother. . . .

Hippolyte resumes talking into the phone.

HIPPOLYTE (*still very friendly*): We're going to shoot Professor Vaugeois, sir. . . . Yes, that's what I said: shoot.

TONIN: And give him a big kiss from me.

HIPPOLYTE: I give you a big kiss, sir. . . . (*To Tonin*) He hung up!

Tonin goes over to Vaugeois. He is holding a bottle of pear brandy in one hand, from which he takes a long swig.

TONIN (*savagely*): So, what is it you plan to tell about Commander Mery, eh?

Vaugeois does not answer. Faure walks over to him with a smile.

FAURE: A man like you, working hand in glove with terrorists! I just don't understand it! . . . Bolshevism in France, is that what you want?

VAUGEOIS (*calmly, with dignity*): I'm a Gaullist, sir!

FAURE (*shrugging*): You can't be serious! Don't you know that De Gaulle is surrounded with Jews and Communists? You don't believe me? You want me to quote some names? . . . Schumann: now try and convince me that's a *French* name. What do you say, Professor?

Tonin makes a gesture that clearly implies that he has no time for such inanities.

TONIN (*to Faure*): Let's save the politics for later. (*Turning to Vaugeois, and speaking in a falsely childish tone*) Come on, Doctor, tell me something about Commander Mery. (*He takes another swig from the bottle.*) Come on, tell me all you know, Doctor!

During this time, Jean-Bernard and Hippolyte are making a tour of the living room, rummaging in the drawers, opening the glass doors of the display cases. Jean-Bernard is pointing out to Hippolyte which objects are of value and worth taking, and the latter stuffs the chosen goods into a big sack he is holding: small statues, jade, silverware.

Lucien is examining the model ocean liner. Timidly, Vaugeois's son moves over toward where Lucien is standing.

LUCIEN: What is it?

VAUGEOIS'S SON: It's the *Wandera*. . . . (*Growing bolder*) I made it myself. It took me a full year. . . .

He runs a finger lovingly over the model. One feels that the ship is his whole life, that he put his heart and soul into it.

VAUGEOIS'S SON (*smiling*): It's almost finished. . . .

LUCIEN: Is it a lot of work?

VAUGEOIS'S SON (*enthusiastically*): Yes. . . . Especially the portholes. . . .

Lucien studies the boy, who is roughly his own age, and who for him is like a Martian. Jean-Bernard joins them near the model. He too runs a finger over the superstructure, the masts. Vaugeois's son makes an instinctive movement, as though to stop him, but thinks better of it and pulls back.

JEAN-BERNARD (*softly*): So, are you like your father? You don't know anything about the underground either?

Jean-Bernard's finger lingers on one of the masts, which suddenly he snaps off with a simple flick. The Vaugeois boy watches him, appalled and fascinated. Lucien moves forward, sticks his finger into one of the portholes, and slowly pulls it up; with an ominous crack, a portion of the deck comes off, and the boy's face fills with a pained expression.

19

Lucien ascends the top steps of the spiral staircase and knocks on Horn's door. We can hear a piano playing. Horn opens the door, and Lucien goes inside. Horn, who is unshaven, is wearing the same dressing gown we have seen him in before, with a silk scarf tied loosely around his neck.

LUCIEN (*unsure of himself*): Good morning. . . .

HORN: Good morning.

Horn heads for a sink in the hallway and washes his hands very meticulously. He is slightly bent over, and looks at himself in the mirror, then runs one of his hands through his hair. Still drying his hands on a towel, he walks back into the room where Lucien is waiting.

HORN: Your suit is ready. . . .

The suit is laid out on the big table next to the couch. Horn points to the bottom of the trousers.

HORN: I made you a pair of golf trousers. It's more elegant for a young man. . . .

Lucien sits down on the couch, lights a cigarette, and places the pack on the table. Then, still looking at Horn, he flicks the pack with his finger and sends it spinning across the table toward Horn. Lucien gestures to Horn as if to say, "Help yourself." Horn extracts a cigarette from the pack without touching the pack itself. Lucien hands him a lighter. Horn takes it, but can't quite manage to light the cigarette, which he finally sets down at random.

HORN: Do you like golf trousers?

Lucien fails to answer. Horn seems embarrassed.

HORN: We can, if you prefer, make a regular pair of trousers. . . . But I find there's something about the

golf trousers, something more, how shall I put it,
more. . . .

Lucien, completely unruffled, goes on smoking his cigarette as
Horn hunts for the perfect analogy.

LUCIEN: Just what are . . . golf trousers?

Horn looks at him without saying anything, but with a fair
degree of astonishment. Lucien straightens up, snuffs out the
cigarette between his fingers, blows on the butt, and puts it in
his pocket.

LUCIEN (threateningly): Just what are golf trousers?

HORN (indicating the bottoms of the trousers): It's . . .
it's when the bottoms are like this. . . .

Horn brings the coat and trousers over to Lucien.

HORN: What we need is a fitting.

Then he goes back over to the sink and washes his hands again.
Meanwhile, Lucien gets up, nonchalantly takes his revolver
from his pocket and places it on the table, where he gives it a
couple of friendly pats, as he would to an animal.
In the background, Horn has his back to Lucien, who
takes off the trousers he has arrived in. He slips into the golf
trousers, whistling softly to himself as he does. He looks down
at the bottoms of the trousers.

LUCIEN: These what you call golf trousers?

HORN (motionless, almost solemn): That's right. That's
what they're called. . . .

Horn bends down to fasten the trousers at the calves.

HORN: Are you a native of the town?

LUCIEN: No, I'm from Souleillac.

HORN: And you're a . . . a friend of Jean-Bernard de
Voisins?

LUCIEN: Yeah.

HORN (*groping*): Are you . . . a student? Are you . . . on vacation?

LUCIEN: No. I work in the German police.

Horn takes the blow with bowed head. Then he gets up and helps Lucien slip into the jacket, to which he makes some minor adjustments. From the table he takes a big pair of tailor's scissors and snips off a few stray ends of thread that still show, especially in the area around the collar. He circles slowly around Lucien, who stands there motionless.

HORN (*as though he were speaking to himself*): The fact is . . . I knew Jean-Bernard's father, the Count de Voisins. . . . A charming man. . . . He used to worry a lot about his son.

Lucien gingerly picks up his revolver, shoves it deep into his inside coat pocket, then takes it out again.

LUCIEN: So it's true, eh . . . you're a Jew?

Horn does not answer. The piano, which we have heard up till now, has stopped.

LUCIEN: Monsieur Faure says that Jews are the enemies of France.

HORN: No . . . not me. . . .

Lucien now tries to fit the revolver into his other pocket.

LUCIEN: Are you from Paris?

HORN: Yes. . . . I was a good tailor. . . . I had a good clientele . . . friends. . . .

Suddenly a girl about twenty enters the room, a smile on her lips. She sees Lucien, looks at him for a moment, then goes toward the hallway. Horn, whose back has been to her, has not seen her. Lucien follows her with his eyes.
She comes back into the room, carrying a shopping bag.

Methodically, with no effort at stealth or speed, she goes over to a drawer and takes out some money, glancing now and then at Lucien with curiosity.

Lucien's eyes are still glued on the girl.

Horn, following Lucien's gaze, turns around and sees her. He seems upset, and takes a step or two in her direction.

HORN: What do you want?

THE GIRL: I'm going out to do some shopping.

HORN: Can't you see I'm busy.

The girl comes over to Lucien.

THE GIRL (*to Horn*): Aren't you going to introduce me?

Horn hesitates a moment.

HORN (*embarrassed, to Lucien*): My daughter.

LUCIEN: What's her name?

HORN: France. . . .

They shake hands and stand looking at each other for a long moment.

Horn takes his daughter by the arm and steers her toward the door.

> HORN (*peremptorily*): Come on, hurry up now. . . . I'll see you in a little while.

She exits. Horn comes back to Lucien, who has gone over to a full-length mirror, in which he is studying himself. He squares his shoulders and slowly buttons the jacket.

> LUCIEN (*without looking at Horn*): Monsieur Jean-Bernard asked me to ask you for the money you owe him.

Horn opens a table drawer and takes out a wad of banknotes, which he counts wearily. He hands the wad to Lucien, who stuffs it in his pocket.

> HORN: Please tell Monsieur Jean-Bernard from me that his father would be very sad if he could see this. . . . He was a real gentleman! . . . (*Then, savagely*) Oh, and besides I don't give a damn!

Lucien has buttoned all the jacket buttons, so that he finds it hard to put his revolver in his inside pocket. He stands there in front of the mirror, looking very solemn and serious.

20

Lucien, wearing his new suit and carrying his old pair of trousers rolled up under his arm, crosses a town square full of life and movement, some of which is very unusual. A dozen or so German soldiers clamber down from a military truck, joking and jostling one another.

Lucien turns into a narrow side street lined with various shops. A passerby glances down at his knickers.

There is a long line of housewives in front of a shop that sells milk and dairy products. Lucien walks past the line, until near the end he sees Horn's daughter. He greets her and she responds. Lucien starts on his way, takes a few steps, pauses, turns around, and comes back to her.

LUCIEN: Come with me.

He takes her by the arm and leads her up to the head of the line. The housewives object and, growing more and more angry, start to use abusive language. Lucien tries to force his way into the dairy, but a woman blocks his path.

WOMAN: Not on your life, kids. Back in the line like everyone else!

The housewives are growing increasingly furious: insults and vituperation rain down on them. Lucien, overwhelmed by the reaction, tries to give as good as he gets, fighting back with his best weapon.

LUCIEN *(shouting)*: Priority! . . . German police!

FRANCE *(to Lucien)*: Don't you think you're going a little far?

A paunchy, middle-aged policeman arrives on the scene and grabs Lucien roughly by the arm.

POLICEMAN: All right, kid! . . . What's this all about anyway?

Lucien wrests his arm free, takes a card from his pocket, and hands it to the policeman, who looks it over carefully.

LUCIEN (*artfully*): German police. . . .

POLICEMAN (*taken aback*): You work with Monsieur Tonin?

LUCIEN: Yeah, that's right. . . .

Feeling somewhat uncomfortable, the policeman hands him back his card.

POLICEMAN: Sorry. I didn't know.

He hurries away like a dog with his tail between his legs. Lucien puts the card back in his pocket, and looks around. He sees that France, without a word, is resuming her former place at the back of the line.

21

Late in the afternoon, Lucien climbs the outside staircase of the house where Horn lives, carrying a cardboard box under his arm. He crosses the garden and passes a woman, who looks prim and proper. The woman shoots a distrustful look at him. Lucien takes a few steps, then turns and looks back at her. The woman has stopped in her tracks and is watching him.

Lucien goes inside and ascends the spiral staircase. When he reaches the door, he pauses; from behind it can be heard loud voices. Lucien listens to what they are saying.

FRANCE (*voice over, very upset*): Why are you always dredging up that old story and throwing it in my face! . . . I've already forgotten it.

HORN (*voice over*): But you're the one who brought it up, not me. . . . You're not going to try and tell me that he was a nice boy. Not after what he did. . . .

FRANCE (*voice over*): Let's change the subject. All this is so far away, and so long ago. Paris, and that whole other world. . . .

HORN (*voice over*): It was just a year ago, my dear. . . .

Lucien rings. The argument ceases immediately. Horn's mother opens the door a crack and remains there, stock still, looking at Lucien.

LUCIEN: Monsieur Horn in?

She doesn't answer. Lucien pushes the door open and walks in.
Horn and his daughter are seated at the table, having dinner. Horn rises. He is wearing the familiar dressing gown.

HORN: What's the matter? What do you want?

LUCIEN (*self-assured*): I've come to see your daughter.

Lucien walks straight over to the table and sets down the box he is carrying. Horn moves over beside his daughter, as though to protect her. He remains standing.

LUCIEN: Good afternoon, Mademoiselle.

France, a slight smile playing about her lips, raises her eyes to Lucien.

FRANCE: Good afternoon.

LUCIEN (*as though he were the master of the house, and Horn the guest*): Have a seat, Monsieur Horn.

Horn sits down beside his daughter. Lucien sits down across from them. Pause. They sit looking at each other, without speaking.

LUCIEN: It's nice and cool in here. Not like it is outside.

Horn's mother, coming from the wide hallway in the right background, arrives, carrying a soup tureen. Horn serves his daughter, and says something in German to his mother, who replies with a long German phrase, then turns and goes back into the hallway. She returns with a plate and silverware, which she sets down savagely in front of Lucien, who looks at her with astonishment. She goes back into the hallway and sits down at a small table, resuming her game of solitaire.

HORN (*to Lucien*): I assume you'll be joining us for dinner?

Lucien nods. He serves himself some soup, and begins to eat peasant style—that is, with his face down close to the bowl. Horn and France steal occasional glances at him. Lucien puts some bread in his soup. He sees that the other two are watching him and, as though he has suddenly remembered the presence of the box he had brought, which is sitting on the table beside him, he starts to open it.

LUCIEN: I brought you a present. . . .

From the box he takes out six bottles of champagne, which he lines up in the middle of the table.

LUCIEN (*pointing to the label with obvious pride*): Champagne from Lousy. . . . Monsieur Jean-Bernard told me that's the best there is. (*To France*) Do you like champagne, mademoiselle?

FRANCE: No. Not tonight.

HORN (*dismally*):   But you do, my dear, you like champagne. . . .

Lucien opens the first bottle without taking any precautions,
while Horn and France look on. The cork pops, and the
champagne gushes out. Lucien looks startled for a moment, then
starts to laugh. He's the only one laughing. Slightly embarrassed,
he pours a glass for France, and then Horn. Then he gets up and
carries the bottle over to where the old lady is sitting, and fills her
teacup with champagne.

LUCIEN: Drink up, grandma, drink up!

She pays no attention to Lucien, gets up, goes over to the sink
and empties the cup of champagne into it, then returns to her
game of solitaire. Lucien comes back and sits down across from
Horn and France.

LUCIEN (*raising his glass*):   What say, Monsieur Horn,
a toast?

Horn raises his glass, but indifferently, as though he has no choice. France makes no move to join them.

> LUCIEN: You really ought to try a glass, mademoiselle. . . .

> FRANCE: Your champagne is warm. And besides, it's a bad vintage. . . .

Horn turns to France.

> HORN: France, this young man is a customer. . . . (*To Lucien*) I'm sorry, but I don't remember your name. . . .

> LUCIEN (*mechanically*): Lacombe, Lucien.

> HORN: Lucien. (*Absently*) A nice name!

Lucien is looking at Horn.

> LUCIEN (*menacingly*): And what about you? Your first name's Albert, right?

> HORN (*taken aback*): Yes . . . Albert.

France looks first at one, then the other, then bursts out laughing. Emboldened, Lucien raises his glass to France.

LUCIEN (*smiling*): Cheers! Here's to you . . . darling.

Lucien pronounces "darling" as though it were some foreign word.

FRANCE: Darling?

She bursts out laughing again, then gets up and leaves the table. Horn tries to steer the conversation in a new direction.

HORN: Are you pleased with the new suit? And the golf trousers?

LUCIEN: Not really, Monsieur Horn.

There is in his voice an undercurrent of menace.

22

Later. It is dark out.

France and Horn are seated side by side on a couch. Lucien is sitting in a leather chair whose upholstery has clearly seen better days.

Lucien is smoking. He snuffs out his cigarette, blows on the blackened end, and puts the butt in his pocket. He takes his glass and downs what is left in it. He seems slightly high. He grabs another bottle of champagne and uncorks it.

LUCIEN (*to Horn*): Do you know Betty Beaulieu?

HORN (*clearly at the end of his rope*): I beg your pardon?

LUCIEN: Betty Beaulieu, Jean-Bernard's girlfriend. (*He takes from his pocket the photo Betty dedicated to him.*) She played in *Night Raid.* . . .

He gets up and hands the photo over to Horn, who studies it.

HORN: No, I don't know her.

LUCIEN (*taking the bottle*): Some more champagne, Monsieur Horn? . . . Let's celebrate. . . .

HORN (*his patience exhausted*): No, no more for me. . . .

LUCIEN: Come on, Albert, it won't hurt you!

He fills Horn's glass. Suddenly France straightens up.

FRANCE: Tell me, just what is it we're celebrating?

Horn takes her hand.

HORN: You ought to go to bed. . . .

LUCIEN (*threateningly*): I forbid you to go to bed . . . darling.

FRANCE: Why do you call me "darling"?

LUCIEN: I don't know.

They stare across at each other, then break out laughing.

FRANCE (*insultingly, to Lucien*): And what did you use to do, before you were in the German police?

LUCIEN: Well, I was a . . . a student. . . .

FRANCE: What kind of student?

Lucien, losing his temper, jumps to his feet.

LUCIEN (*threateningly*): You know that I (*pointing to himself*) can have you all arrested. . . .

Horn bends over to France.

HORN: France, shut up!

FRANCE: Are you afraid of him?

LUCIEN: Yes. And he's right to be. . . .

Just then, the doorbell rings. Lucien makes a move to answer it, but Horn gets up quickly.

HORN: I'll go.

Lucien and France are left alone in the room. We hear frag-
ments of a conversation taking place on the stairway, but
without being able to make out the tenor. Lucien looks at
France, who returns his stare. He fills his glass with champagne
and hands it over to her. She raises the glass to her lips and
goes on staring at him, with an expression that is both dreamy
and amused. She runs her fingers lightly over the back of his
hand.

FRANCE: You have funny hands. . . .

Horn comes back into the room, accompanied by a middle-
aged, balding man in a dark suit of the type worn by persons of
distinction in provincial towns.

THE MAN (*with disdainful irony*): But the fact is, my
dear fellow, I have every legal right in the world to raise
your rent. . . . I'm taking enough risks as it is, having
you here in the first place. . . . If you don't like it, no
one is forcing you to stay, you know. France isn't one big
waiting room. . . .

HORN (*wearily*): All right, Monsieur Raverdy.

THE MAN (*disdainfully*): Do you know what the Marshal
said? . . .

Lucien shrugs his shoulders.

LUCIEN (*full of contempt*): The Marshal. . . . (*To
France*) Monsieur Tonin calls him the Old Asshole.
(*He laughs.*)

The man gives Lucien a withering look.

THE MAN: Very funny! (*Turning to Horn*) This gentleman is your guest?

Lucien very slowly gets to his feet, takes out his revolver, and
points it at the man.

LUCIEN: German police!

Dumfounded, the man turns to Horn for clarification.

THE MAN: What's this, some kind of joke?

Horn looks at the man with an air of resignation.

HORN: No. This young man indeed belongs to the German police.

Lucien extends his left arm to the man and snaps his fingers.

LUCIEN: Your papers! . . .

The man hesitates a moment, then hands Lucien his identity papers, looking very much at this point like a sleepwalker.

Lucien examines the papers from every possible angle, sniffs them, then lets them fall to the floor. The man stoops down and picks them up.

LUCIEN: Get out!

The man leaves the room, followed by Horn. As he reaches the door he turns back.

THE MAN (*under his breath*): So, you entertain members of the Gestapo! Congratulations!

23

Much later. Horn is still sitting on the couch. Lucien is pacing the floor. He walks over to the hallway, then turns around, pointing to the door at the far end.

LUCIEN: Is that where your daughter sleeps?

Horn, dead with fatigue, yawns.

HORN: Yes, that's where she sleeps. . . .

LUCIEN (*loudly*): Then we ought to speak softly, so we won't wake her up.

HORN (*mechanically, beyond impatience*): Yes.

Lucien comes back to the table and pours some more champagne into Horn's glass. Then he pours himself some, which he downs in a single gulp. He sits down.

LUCIEN: By the way, Albert, your daughter is pretty.

Horn doesn't answer. He seems physically and mentally exhausted.

LUCIEN: But how come you two argue so much?

Horn shrugs.

HORN: France and I get along very well.

LUCIEN: I didn't want to say it in front of her . . . but the other day I killed a guy. (*He simulates shooting a revolver.*) Bang! . . .

Horn does not react. Lucien leans over to him.

LUCIEN: You know, Albert . . . You shouldn't believe everything Monsieur Jean-Bernard tells you. All those stories about Spain. . . . (*Pause.*) He's only after your money, Albert. . . .

HORN: Do you think I didn't know it?

24

A deep, narrow valley, cut off at the far end by a steep cliff. Silence, and a general impression of heat and torpor.

Suddenly the silence is broken by the sound of submachine-gun fire, first a single burst, then several, and the sound of explosions of different intensities and sources.

Twenty or so members of the Militia start up the hill, attacking the cliff. Halfway up the cliff is a cave, in front of which the members of the underground have set up a single field piece.

Among the members of the advancing Militia we recognize Tonin, Aubert, Hippolyte, and Lucien. Lucien catches sight of a rabbit bounding away not far from him. He turns from the battle in progress and fires a burst of his submachine gun after the fleeing rabbit, but misses it. He hears a burst of fire from the underground's gun position, followed almost immediately by a scream.

HIPPOLYTE (*shouting*): The boss! The boss! They got the boss!

Lucien turns around and sees Tonin on the ground, perched on one elbow, holding his right shoulder.

TONIN (*grimacing*): Goddamnit! Just my damn luck! . . .

Hippolyte, helped by Lucien, pulls Tonin to his feet, supporting him by the left shoulder. Together, they move Tonin down the slope. Aubert is waiting for them partway down the hill.

AUBERT (*terrified*): It doesn't hurt too much, does it, Pierre?

TONIN: I only hope they didn't hit the lung.

AUBERT: Don't worry, Pierre!

TONIN: You don't have anything to drink?

Aubert takes out a flask and hands it to Tonin, who takes a long swig. Lucian follows behind, carrying his submachine gun.

AUBERT (*to Tonin*): I told you, Pierre! I told you we should have left this job to the Militia!

HIPPOLYTE: Don't worry, boss, everything's going to be all right!

25

Night. A black Citroën pulls up in front of Horn's house and stops. Lucien, carrying a small suitcase in one hand and his submachine gun in the other, gets out.

LUCIEN (*thickly*): 'Night!

AUBERT (*voice over*): Good luck!

The car pulls away, and Lucien goes into the house.

When he reaches the top of the spiral staircase, he rings Horn's doorbell, several long rings. Finally the door opens and Horn appears, wearing silk pajamas.

HORN: What do you want?

Lucien points his gun at Horn's midsection, holding it with one hand as he goes "Ta-ta-ta-ta-ta," imitating the sound of gun fire. Then he goes into the room, sets his suitcase on the table, and turns to Horn.

LUCIEN: They shot my boss.

HORN: What?

LUCIEN (*threateningly*): Your friends . . . they wounded my boss!

HORN: What friends?

LUCIEN: The Bolsheviks. . . . (*Suddenly switching subjects*) Can I . . . can I see . . . France?

Horn remains motionless, without replying. Lucien heads for the room at the end of the hallway and pushes open the door. He goes into the room and stands there for a moment, gazing down at France asleep. He is still holding his gun in his hand. France opens her eyes and looks up at him. Lucien comes back into the other room and opens the suitcase, which contains banknotes, silverware, and a wide variety of other objects, including a bottle of cognac.

LUCIEN: You see, Albert. . . . Spoils of war. . . .

From the suitcase he takes a heavy gold pocket watch and, holding it by its chain, reaches over and slips it into Horn's pajama pocket. Horn doesn't bat an eyelash. Lucien stares vacantly at Horn, and there seems to be a trace of sadness in his eyes.

LUCIEN (*murmuring*): France. . . .

HORN: You ought to go home and go to bed. . . .

He closes Lucien's suitcase and hands it to Lucien, who brings his fingers to his temple in a mock salute.

LUCIEN (*backing away*): France. . . . Long live France, Albert. . . . Long live France!

Lucien is walking rather clumsily down a deserted street, his suitcase in one hand, the submachine gun in the other. A strong impression of loneliness.

26

Evening. Lucien is walking through the garden that leads to the Horns'. He is dressed in a new suit, this one with normal trousers. In his hand he holds a bouquet of flowers.

Horn's mother opens the door. Lucien hands her the bouquet.

LUCIEN: Here. It's for you. . . .

Horn's mother does not react to Lucien's gesture, and for several embarrassed seconds he stands there holding the bouquet. Then he goes into the main room. No one is there, but from the adjoining room can be heard the sound of the piano, which drifts through the partly opened door.

Lucien heads for the door and goes into the next room. France is playing the piano. Behind her, seated on a chair, Horn is listening with rapt attention, in a classic pose: his head is slightly bowed, and he holds two fingers to his temple. When Lucien comes into the room, he turns his head ever so slightly, then returns to his position of contemplation. France goes on playing. Lucien stands there, listening, the bouquet of flowers in his hands. France is playing the last movement of Beethoven's "Moonlight" sonata. When she has finished, Horn turns to Lucien.

HORN: That music is sad, don't you find?

Lucien doesn't know what to do with his bouquet of flowers.

LUCIEN: Yes.

HORN: And you know: I have the feeling that my whole life has been lived in time to that music. . . .

France puts her hand on her father's arm.

FRANCE (*solicitously*): You're not going to start in on that again, Father. . . . (*To Lucien*) Good evening.

LUCIEN (*embarrassed*): 'Evening.

Horn struggles to his feet.

HORN: France is a very fine pianist. . . . She should have gone to the Conservatory . . (*He sighs.*) But then. . . .

FRANCE: Please, Father!

Suddenly, Lucien thrusts his bouquet toward Horn.

LUCIEN: Here . . . I . . . I brought you some flowers.

Astonished, Horn accepts the flowers.

LUCIEN (*solemnly and self-consciously*): Monsieur Horn, I have come to fetch your daughter. . . .

HORN (*holding the bouquet of flowers*): What?

LUCIEN (*smiling*): Jean-Bernard and Betty are leaving tomorrow morning. . . . It's their farewell party tonight. I'd like to invite France. . . .

HORN: Are you crazy?

LUCIEN (*menacingly*): Not really, Monsieur Horn.

HORN: France is very tired.

Still looking at Horn, Lucien puts his hand on France's shoulder.

LUCIEN: If she doesn't come with me, I'll take you in her place!

A moment's silence. Lucien sits down on the piano keyboard, provoking a cacophony of notes.

LUCIEN: There are some people down there who aren't fond of Jews, Monsieur Horn!

France gets up, shrugging her shoulders.

FRANCE: I'm going with him. . . .

Horn tries to restrain her, to assert his parental authority.

HORN (*holding her arm*): I forbid you!

France gives him a kiss on the forehead.

FRANCE: Don't be silly, Father. . . .

LUCIEN: And don't take all day getting ready. We'll be late. . . .

France leaves the room.

Horn and Lucien remain behind, Horn looking distressed and lost, still holding the bouquet in one hand. Again Lucien sits down on the keyboard, provoking another discord of sound.

27

Late at night, at the bar of the hotel, the party is in full swing, with lots of couples dancing. Lucien is alone at one table. Betty, who was dancing, comes back to where Lucien is sitting and tries to pull him out onto the dance floor.

BETTY: Come on and dance, Lucien!

Lucien holds back.

LUCIEN: I don't know how.

BETTY (*disappointed*): You have to learn, Lucien!

She goes back out onto the dance floor, twisting and turning as she dances alone, her skirt swirling as she turns.

Jean-Bernard, who has been dancing with France, brings her back to the table. He is wiping his face with a handkerchief. France takes her empty champagne glass and hands it over to Jean-Bernard, who fills it for her.

FRANCE: I'm hot.

She empties the glass in one gulp.

LUCIEN (*dryly*): It's getting late. . . . I should be taking you home.

France looks at him, a half-smile playing on her lips.

FRANCE: You're a strange duck, Lucien. . . .

Aubert, walking unsteadily, comes to the table and leans over close to France.

> AUBERT (*with exaggerated good manners*): You look as though you were bored. . . . Would you be so kind as to grant me this dance?

France, after a glance at Lucien, gets up and follows him. They start to dance. France dances very well indeed.

Jean-Bernard and Lucien, who are seated side by side, watch them.

> JEAN-BERNARD (*dreamily*): She's very pretty, that girl. . . .

He turns to Lucien.

> JEAN-BERNARD: You'll say good-bye for me to Papa Horn. . . . If he asks you about Spain (*laughing*), simply tell him that I left in his place. . . . (*He gives a deep sigh.*) If you knew how the whole thing bores me. . . .

Lucien isn't listening to him. He's still looking at France danc-ing with Aubert, who is holding her close and whispering in her ear. France breaks into a smile. Jean-Bernard is also watching them.

> JEAN-BERNARD (*still musing*): There are some Jewish girls who are incredibly beautiful. . . . Compared to them, other women look like mares. . . . (*Turning to Lucien*) That's right, old boy: mares. . . . I had a Jewish fiancée once, some time back. . . . Incredibly stacked, and incredibly wealthy. . . .

Betty, who looks worn out, comes back to the table.

> BETTY: What is it you're telling Lucien, Jean, baby?

> JEAN-BERNARD (*wearily*): Nothing, darling, nothing.

Lucien looks back out at the dance floor. Now Aubert is not only holding France very close, but his hand is groping her buttocks as he tries to kiss her. Lucien gets up, stalks out onto the floor, takes France by the arm, and pulls her violently away. Aubert stands there looking at him. There is a moment of ten-sion, as people stop talking and look at the confrontation, which might easily degenerate into a fight. But Aubert, staggering, starts to laugh and claps Lucien affectionately on the shoulder. Lucien, dragging France behind him, walks through the bar and heads toward the hotel entrance. She stumbles, and Lucien has to catch her to prevent her from falling.

> FRANCE: You made me break my heel!

She sits down on the bottom step of the stairway, holding her shoe in her hand. The stairway and entrance hall are in semi-darkness. A sentry is sprawled on a chair, half-asleep, a sub-machine gun across his knees. France examines her shoes, rubs her heel, all the while looking at Lucien with a dreamy smile.

> FRANCE: Can we use the familiar form of address, Lu-cien? Stop being so formal?

Lucien doesn't answer.

Betty's Great Dane comes over and begins to sniff France and Lucien. France begins to pet him.

LUCIEN (*with irritation*): You drank too much. I have to take you home.

He shifts his weight back and forth from one foot to the other, looking very impatient. She studies him.

FRANCE: It's a shame you don't know how to dance. . . . (*She gets up.*) I'm going to teach you.

She takes off her other shoe and, to the strains of the music coming from the bar, begins to dance with him. Lucien, very uptight, takes a few tentative steps, trying to follow her.

FRANCE: Relax. . . . You'll see how easy it is. . . .

Lucien catches sight of Marie, who appears from the direction of the bar and makes a beeline for them. They stop dancing when she plants herself squarely in front of them.

MARIE (*softly*): I should have suspected . . . you really took me in. . . .

Lucien takes a step toward Marie.

MARIE (*hissing*): You bastard! You lousy son of a bitch!

She tries to slap him, but he catches her arm. She wrenches herself free.

MARIE (*pointing to France*): Aubert told me her father's a Jew! . . . She has no right coming here. . . .

She takes a menacing step toward France.

MARIE: Dirty Jew!

France backs up, staring fixedly at Marie.

MARIE: Dirty Jew!

Lucien takes Marie by the arm and leads her back toward the bar. She twists around so that she is facing him. Her voice is growing shriller and shriller. The sentry has straightened up, and several people, including Jean-Bernard, appear at the entrance of the bar, to see what's going on.

MARIE: So, you're sleeping with a Jewess! . . . And you think you can get away with it? Oh, no you won't. I'm going to fetch the krauts. Right this minute!

Jean-Bernard comes over to Marie and, with a charming smile, takes her by the waist.

JEAN-BERNARD: Don't get so excited, Marie, dear. It's not as serious as all that. . . .

He leads her over toward the bar. Marie resists and, still turning back to Lucien, continues screaming at the top of her lungs:

> MARIE: Dirty Jew! . . . They all have the syph! . . . Do you hear that? . . . She's going to give you a case of syph!

Lucien, who remains impassive, listens to Marie's voice as she is led away.

> MARIE (*voice over*): Let me go. . . . I haven't finished what I had to say to that little bitch. . . . She has no right to set foot in here. . . . Let me go, I tell you. . . .

Lucien turns around, looking for France, who has disappeared. The sentry, who is still seated in the same chair, motions up the stairs with his gun. Lucien races up after her.

28

When he reaches the second story landing, Lucien glances down the hallway, but it's empty. *The door to the large bathroom where the interrogations take place is ajar, however, and Lucien goes inside. France is on her knees next to the bathtub, her head on the edge, as though she were throwing up. Her body is racked with sobs, her breathing labored, as though she is suffocating. Lucien sits down on the edge of the bathtub, not quite knowing what to do. Then he kneels down beside her. She looks at him: her face is bathed in tears. She grabs hold of Lucien, tightly, and buries her head on his shoulder. Her whole body is still shaken with convulsive sobs. Lucien, upset and awkward, caresses her hair.*

> LUCIEN (*to fill the silence*): I don't understand. . . . Usually Marie's very sweet. . . .

France lifts her head and looks at Lucien intently.

> FRANCE (*like a little child*): Lucien . . . I'm so tired. I can't stand it any more. . . . I'm so tired of being a Jew. . . .

France's arms are around Lucien's neck. She clings to him closely, convulsively, as though she were drowning. She begins to kiss him with a kind of desperate fury: on the neck, the cheeks, the lips.

29

Dawn.

France, who is naked, is curled up on the small couch. Lucien, who is seated on the floor beside her, watches her and lightly caresses her back and buttocks, ever so gently, the way one would pet an animal. From somewhere outside, we hear the sound of doors being opened, then Betty's familiar laughter. Lucien gets up and walks over to the window, which looks out onto the courtyard below.

He sees Jean-Bernard and Betty getting into the Delahaye. Aubert, who is very drunk, still has a glass in his hand. He leans over the car door and gives Betty a kiss. The car starts away. Betty waves and Aubert lifts his glass in a morning toast.

BETTY: We'll send you some postcards from Spain!

Lucien comes back over to France, who is now awake and sitting up with her knees pulled up to her chin. Lucien sits down be-

side her, takes her neck, and pulls her close to him. She looks up at him.

> FRANCE: Lucien. . . . (*Pause.*) Lucien. . . . My father has to be taken to Spain. . . .

She snuggles up against him, the way a little girl would.

30

Two similar-looking Citroën sedans are driving along a two-lane highway at top speed. We can see that Aubert is at the wheel of one of the cars, with Lucien in the front seat beside him, a machine gun on his knees. As they round a curve, they come upon the Delahaye athwart the road, its doors wide open. The occupants of the two Citroëns hurry out of their cars and find, sprawled on the shoulders of the road, first Jean-Bernard, then Betty, both dead, both killed with what must have been submachine-gun fire.

Slightly farther along, the Great Dane lies wounded but still breathing with difficulty. Lucien and the other members of the German police look on without exchanging a word.

31

At the Horn's place. Afternoon. Horn is seated at the table of the main room, sewing the buttons on a vest. In the hallway Horn's mother is busy doing something at the two-burner stove. From the next room, we can hear intermittent bits and pieces of piano music being played, but nothing sustained.

Horn is wearing his pajamas. Lucien is watching him sew.

LUCIEN: It's funny, your knowing how to sew and all, Monsieur Horn. . . .

Horn does not respond.

LUCIEN (*with no malice intended*): Usually, it's the women who do the sewing, no? . . . (*Pause.*) Cat got your tongue, Monsieur Horn?

Still no reply. Lucien heads for the room where the piano is. He sees France, whose back is to him, seated at the piano, picking out a few notes. She turns briefly, looks at him absently, then goes back to her playing. Lucien returns to the main room. Horn gets up, goes over, and closes the door between the two rooms, as though he wanted to isolate France. Then he slips on the vest he has been working on over his pajamas and inspects it in the tall mirror.

Lucien opens the door between the two rooms, then turns to Horn.

LUCIEN: And what would you say if I married France?

Horn stiffens, stands there for a moment without moving a muscle, then turns and looks Lucien up and down.

HORN (*musing*): It's strange, somehow I can't bring myself to loathe you completely. . . .

Someone knocks at the door.
Horn goes over and opens it. It is Hippolyte, accompanied by a woman in her Sunday best: Lucien's mother.

HIPPOLYTE (*to Horn*): A visitor for Monsieur Lacombe.

Horn doesn't appear to understand.

HIPPOLYTE (*pointing to Thérèse*): This is Lucien's mother.

They both come into the room. Lucien has come over to them.

THÉRÈSE (*embarrassed*): Lucien. . . .

LUCIEN: Hello.

Horn, who seems surprised, looks at them.

HIPPOLYTE (*to Lucien*): Your mother came looking for

you at the hotel. . . . So I brought her over here. I thought I was doing the right thing. . . .

A silence. Lucien looks at his mother.

HIPPOLYTE (*turning to Thérèse and Horn*): Good-bye, now.

He leaves, closing the door behind him.

THÉRÈSE (*embarrassed*): He's a very kind man. . . .

HORN (*gesturing toward the center of the room*): Please come in.

He seats her on the couch and sits down in a chair opposite her. Lucien, obviously upset by the unexpected visit, also takes a seat. In the next room, the sound of the piano can be heard again. Horn turns to his mother, who has stopped her puttering in the kitchen and is standing on the threshold of the main room, and utters a long sentence in German. Thérèse and Lucien exchange glances.

HORN (*to Thérèse*): I'm sorry to receive you like this, Madame. . . . (*He runs a hand over the vest he is wearing.*) Did you come a long way?

THÉRÈSE: From Soulcillac.

LUCIEN (*dryly, to Horn*): That's our village.

Horn's mother crosses the room, carrying a tray with two cups on it. One she hands to Thérèse, the other to Horn.

HORN (*to his mother, nodding to Thérèse*): Das ist die Mutter von Lucien. . . .

The old lady's normally impassive face has a brief but ambiguous expression as she bows her head slightly in Thérèse's direction.

THÉRÈSE (*impressed*): How do you do, Madame?

The old woman walks back to the hallway-kitchen without responding verbally. Nervously, Lucien lights a cigarette. Thérèse seems embarrassed, not quite knowing what to do with her cup of tea.

THÉRÈSE (*to Lucien*): Laborit had to come in for the fair . . . so I came with him.

LUCIEN: I see. . . .

THÉRÈSE (*very solemnly*): You know, you won't be able to come back to the village any more.

Lucien shrugs his shoulders.

LUCIEN (*to his mother*): Did you receive the money orders?

THÉRÈSE: Yes.

She bends over and opens her oversize handbag.

THÉRÈSE: Here, I brought you a chicken. . . .

LUCIEN (*taking the chicken*): Thanks.

THÉRÈSE: Are you getting enough to eat?

LUCIEN (*embarrassed*): Yes.

He doesn't know what to do with the chicken. Finally he gets up and takes it over to Horn's mother.

During the above exchange, Horn has been watching them, gravely and silently. The piano has stopped.

France comes into the room, and walks over toward the couch. Horns gets up. He indicates Thérèse.

HORN: This is Lucien's mother. . . .

France nods and extends her hand to Thérèse.

HORN (*to Thérèse*): My daughter. . . .

Lucien is smoking his cigarette. France sits down beside him.

THÉRÈSE (*to Horn, trying to be friendly*): Your daughter's very pretty. . . .

Horn does not reply. A general feeling of embarrassment.
Thérèse gets up.

THÉRÈSE (*to Lucien*): You know, I only meant to stop by to thank you for the money orders. . . . But I don't want to intrude. . . .

HORN: I assure you, you're not intruding, Madame.

Thérèse, not quite sure what to do next, sits down again. A pause. She turns to Horn:

THÉRÈSE: Are you from these parts?

HORN: No. We're . . . we're from Paris. . . . But Paris has become, how shall I say, very difficult to live in. . . .

THÉRÈSE (*smiling*): Because there's nothing to eat up there? (*Pause.*) You're not French, are you?

HORN: More or less. . . . My daughter is *really* French.

THÉRÈSE (*seemingly reassured*): Oh, good. . . . Does she like it here?

HORN: Ask her.

THÉRÈSE: Lucien should take her around and show her the sights. . . . (*Without thinking*) The only thing is, he can't come back to the village any more. . . .

There are a few seconds of embarrassed silence.

THÉRÈSE (*to Horn, very openly*): Oh, if you must know, I worry a lot about Lucien. . . .

HORN: I do too, Madame.

THÉRÈSE: And yet, he's not a bad boy. You're a friend of Lucien's; maybe you can talk some sense into him. . . .

HORN: I'm not a friend of Lucien's.

Throughout this whole conversation, Lucien and France have remained silent, like two children following the grownups' conversation.

HORN (*after a few seconds*): I worry a great deal about my daughter too. . . . A great deal. . . .

THÉRÈSE: Really?

Thérèse stares fixedly at Horn. Then she lapses into silence.

HORN (*sadly*): I wonder what her mother would say if she could see her now. . . .

THÉRÈSE: Where is her mother?

Horn doesn't answer. Another silence. Finally:

HORN: Don't you find, Madame, that we were all better off before the war?

32

Lucien and his mother emerge from the porte-cochere of the Horn house. They take a few steps and come out onto a small square. Thérèse stops.

THÉRÈSE: Well, I suppose. . . .

LUCIEN: I'm going to walk you to your bus.

THÉRÈSE (*with animation*): Don't bother. It's better Laborit doesn't lay eyes on you. . . .

A pause. Thérèse has a moment's hesitation, then:

THÉRÈSE: Do you know what I received, because of you?

From her pocket she takes a miniature black coffin and hands it to Lucien, who takes it and turns it over in his hand.

LUCIEN: It's nothing. . . . Here we receive them every day of the week.

THÉRÈSE: They're going to kill you, Lucien. . . . Labont says that they're going to kill you. . . . Why don't you run away, go some place where they don't know you? . . .

Lucien hesitates, as though he were thinking. Then he shrugs.

LUCIEN: I like it here where I am. . . .

Pause.

THÉRÈSE: All right, well. . . . I'm going to miss my bus. . . .

They embrace awkwardly. Suddenly Thérèse seems anxious to be off.

LUCIEN: Wait. . . .

From his pocket he takes a wad of money and presses it into her hand. She looks at the wad.

THÉRÈSE (*with embarrassment*): Thanks.

She turns and leaves. The square is virtually deserted. Lucien stands there motionless, watching her move away. At one point she turns around and smiles back at him.

33

It is evening, and Horn, France, and Lucien are seated at the table of the main room. Lucien and France are on one side, with Horn across from them. Horn's mother brings a tray of food, puts it down on the table, then returns to her own table as is her custom. Lucien eats voraciously. Horn, who seems lost in his thoughts, is smoking a cigarette, using a cigarette holder. He doesn't flick the ashes off but carefully deposits them in the ashtray.

FRANCE: You ought to eat something, Father.

HORN (*without raising his voice*): It's very hard to be hungry when your daughter is a whore. . . .

He gets to his feet and crosses to his mother, to whom he speaks harshly in German, as though he were taking out his anger on her. Horn's mother answers her son in the same tone, as France and Lucien listen silently.

Taking advantage of a break in the Horns' conversation, Lucien comes to France's defense.

LUCIEN: That wasn't very nice, what you said to France, Monsieur Horn. . . .

Horn comes back over to where Lucien is sitting and stands towering over him. For a moment, one has the impression he is going to hit Lucien. Lucien moves back in his chair and looks up at Horn with a smile.

LUCIEN: If you ask me, Monsieur Horn, I find calling your own daughter a whore vulgar. . . . You deserve a good licking. . . .

HORN (*disdainfully, looking Lucien up and down*): I

don't need you, sir, to tell me how I should treat my daughter. . . . Anyway, we're alike, France and I. We're both very fragile creatures. . . .

He sits back down, as though exhausted. France takes his hand in hers as she would a child's.

FRANCE: Father. . . .

Horn, his head bowed, does not respond.

France buries her head in her arms and starts to sob. Horn reaches over and begins gently caressing her hair.

HORN: I'm sorry, my love. . . .

Solemnly, Lucien puts his arm around France's shoulders. She frees herself.

FRANCE (*fiercely*): Leave me alone! . . .

Lucien shrugs, gets up, and walks over to the hallway. "Shuffles" would be more accurate, for he seems uncertain what to do next, or where he should go. He pauses for a moment next to Horn's mother, who is busy with her game of solitaire. He enters the

room at the end of the hallway. Horn's bathrobe is lying on the bed. Whistling, Lucien undresses, slips into the bathrobe, then goes back out into the hallway. He sits down at the bridge table across from Horn's mother. Lucien looks bored; he tries to catch the old lady's attention, but she refuses even to glance at him, going on with her game of cards as though he weren't there. Lucien places his hands flat on the table, and lays his chin on them, still watching the old lady from this new position.

Meanwhile, in the main room, France and Horn are still talking softly. We cannot make out what they are saying, except at one moment when Horn, in his irritation, raises his voice.

HORN: Spain! Spain! I tell you, Spain does not exist!

FRANCE (*peremptorily*): Come now, Father, be reasonable. . . .

Lucien goes back over to where they are sitting, takes an apple from the table, and starts to polish it on the bathrobe.

LUCIEN (*still standing, to Horn*): You feeling better?

HORN (*upset*): Yes . . . yes. . . .

Lucien, who has taken up a position directly behind France, puts a hand on her shoulder. He leans over to Horn.

> LUCIEN (*sincerely*): You know, Monsieur Horn, I'm really fond of you. . . .

> HORN (*absently*): Really?

France looks up at Lucien, as though he were bothering her. She removes his hand from her shoulder, leans forward toward her father, and continues talking softly.

> FRANCE (*in a near whisper*): You mustn't talk that way, Father. . . .

Lucien, who feels left out, drums his fingers loudly on the table.

> LUCIEN: I'm going to bed. . . .

He taps Horn on the shoulder.

> LUCIEN: 'Night, everybody.

He leaves the room and disappears down the hallway, leaving Horn and his daughter still carrying on their murmured conversation.

34

Morning. In the hallway kitchen Lucien pours some milk into a large bowl. He is standing next to the stove; Horn's mother is seated at the table. Lucien, carrying a piece of sugar between his fingers as though they were sugar tongs, walks over and drops the sugar into the old lady's cup. She has no reaction. Lucien enters the main room just as Horn is arriving through the front door. Horn is dressed in an impeccable suit and tie. He has shaved too. As he removes his hat, we see that his hair is neatly combed. Lucien goes over to him.

> LUCIEN (*in astonishment*): You been out?

HORN: Yes. . . . A short constitutional through the town. I haven't set foot outdoors for a long time. (*With icy irony*) The old boy's getting his second wind. . . .

He sits down on the couch. Lucien stares at him.

HORN: France told me that you might be able to get us through to Spain. . . .

LUCIEN (*amazed*): Me?

HORN: Yes, you. (*A pause, as though his mind were on other things.*) Lucien, I think it's time you and I had a man-to-man talk. We've never really had a chance to talk together. . . .

Lucien has sat down in order to tie his shoelaces.

LUCIEN: Talk about what?

HORN: About France.

LUCIEN (*getting up*): I don't have time, Monsieur Horn. . . . I have to go to work.

He glances at his watch.

35

Late in the afternoon, two Citroën sedans covered with mud pull up and park in front of the Grotto Hotel. Lucien, Aubert, and two militiamen emerge from one car, Faure from the other. In the back of the second car lies the maimed and disfigured body of a man in civilian clothes, whom the militiamen have trouble getting out of the car. Aubert and Lucien pause for a second to watch the operation.

AUBERT: They really did him in good. . . . (*To Lucien*) I'm dead. . . . I'm going to take a shower.

He goes up the stairs and into the hotel.

36

Lucien is standing in the hotel entranceway, looking toward the bar. On one of the barstools sits a man with a hat, whose back is to Lucien. Behind the bar stands Hippolyte. Lucien walks into the bar and is greeted by Hippolyte with a smile.

HIPPOLYTE: Hey, Lucien. There's a gentleman here wants to talk with you. . . .

Slowly the man at the bar turns around: it is Horn.

LUCIEN (*completely taken aback*): What the hell are you doing here?

HORN: Waiting for you. I was chatting with your friend here. . . . A very nice fellow, really.

On the top of the bar are two glasses, one belonging to Horn, the other to Hippolyte.

HIPPOLYTE (*winking at Lucien*): Another round, monsieur?

Lucien comes closer to Horn.

> LUCIEN: You crazy or something?

> HORN: I told you we had to talk. Quietly. . . . Things can't go on this way. . . .

Lucien takes him by the lapel of his coat and shakes him.

> LUCIEN: You can't help it, can you! You couldn't help acting like a jerk!

Hippolyte watches the scene, his eyes growing wider.

> LUCIEN: Come on! Hurry up! I'm taking you home! . . .

He shoves him toward the entrance of the hotel, where suddenly Horn finds himself literally face to face with Faure, who has just arrived from the courtyard.

> FAURE (*to Lucien, pointing to Horn*): Who's this?

> LUCIEN (*dryly*): A friend of mine. . . .

Horn doffs his hat and introduces himself as though he were in some formal salon.

HORN: Albert Horn, sir.

FAURE (*scrounging in his mental files*): Horn. . . . (*Pause.*) Why . . . you're the Jew!

He turns to Lucien.

FAURE: So, now you're bringing Jews, just like that, to the hotel bar?

HORN (*to Faure*): Don't be too hard on him. He's just a boy, you know. . . .

FAURE (*to Horn*): As for you, come with me into my office!

37

They move into the office. Faure sits down where Lucienne usually sits. Horn is sitting stiffly across from him, with Lucien standing slightly behind him.

FAURE (*scarcely able to conceal his pleasure*): Let me see your papers!

Horn hands him an ID card.

FAURE (*falsely unctuous*): What in the world is this? Jean-François Rivière, born July 30, 1892, in Paris. . . . Was it de Voisins who palmed this off on you?

HORN: It was.

Faure tears the identity card up into tiny pieces.

FAURE: What I want to see is an ID card stamped with the word *Jew*.

HORN (*very calmly*): All I have is a visiting card, sir.

From his inside pocket, Horn takes a visiting card and places it carefully on the table. Faure takes it and begins to type.

FAURE (*typing*): Surname: H-O-R-N. . . . First name: Albert. . . . Born in? . . .

HORN: Szakestahervar. . . .

FAURE: How's that again?

HORN: Why don't you simply put Toulouse?

FAURE (*typing*): Residence?

HORN: Fifty-two, rue Pierre Premier de Serbie, Paris.

Faure goes on typing.

FAURE: Nationality?

HORN: French.

FAURE (*smiling*): Didn't anyone ever tell you that Hebes couldn't be French?

HORN: Occasionally.

Faure settles back in his chair.

FAURE: In my mind a Jew is like a rat, no better, no worse.

HORN (*worried*): You really think so?

FAURE: You bet I do! (*He makes a gesture.*) They breed like crazy. . . . (*With a faraway expression*) There're more and more of them every day. . . .

HORN: If you like I can leave.

FAURE: Stay right where you are! I'm going to call the Kommandantur! You'll do your explaining to them, pal. . . .

HORN (*with surprise*): What gives you license to speak with such familiarity to me?

Faure takes the telephone and starts to call.

FAURE: Hello! Hello! I'd like to speak to Officer Müller. . . . Hello. . . .

*It becomes obvious that no one on the other end of the line
speaks French. Faure tries to speak a sentence or two of German.
His accent is terrible.*

Lucien takes a step or two closer to Horn.

LUCIEN: Monsieur Horn. . . .

Horn looks up at him.

HORN: We never had a chance to talk about France.
. . . She was asleep when I left. . . . (*Pause.*) What I
wanted to say to you, Lucien. . . .

*He doesn't have a chance to finish his sentence. While he has
been talking to Lucien, Faure has managed to get through to the
German officer he was trying to reach.*

FAURE (*wittily*): Hello. . . . You'll never guess, my dear
friend, who I have sitting here in my office. A Jew . . .
a real live Jew.

38

Lucien, who appears very nervous and turns to glance
back over his shoulder several times, is walking in the direction
of Horn's house. There are few people in the street, and at one
point Lucien has the impression that a man is following him.
The midday silence is punctuated with the sound of a news
bulletin coming over the radio, and some snatches of music.
Lucien ducks into a porte-cochere, turns, waits, and takes his
revolver from his pocket.

A man, who seems to be looking for something or someone, passes the door. He glances in the direction of Lucien,
who springs out, pointing the gun at the man as he checks his
jacket pockets to make sure he isn't armed. The man seems
terrified. Lucien looks at him for a moment, then shrugs his
shoulders and says, as he gives him a shove, "Keep moving," the
way a cop would.

Standing on the top steps of the spiral staircase before the
Horns' front door, Lucien is ringing the bell, over and over

again. Horn's mother finally appears, but as soon as she sees Lucien she closes the door again. Lucien, knocking wildly on the door, starts to shout, louder and louder:

LUCIEN: Open up. Open up for the love of God!

But the door is very solid and there is no way Lucien is going to break it down. Furious, he takes out his revolver and is preparing to shoot off the lock, when the door opens again, as though the old lady had been able to see what he was about to do. Lucien, somewhat abashed, finds himself standing in front of the old lady with a gun in his hand.

LUCIEN: Old witch! Where's France?

Without replying, Horn's mother turns her back to Lucien. Lucien enters the apartment, goes through the hallway, and heads directly for the door at the end of it. France is sitting on the bed. Her eyes follow Lucien as he comes in, but she says nothing. He sits down on the bed beside her, but she straightens up, then gets up and goes over to the window.

LUCIEN (*softly*): They've taken him away. . . . I don't

know where. . . . It's his own fault. . . . There was
nothing I could do. . . .

FRANCE (*violently*): Shut up!

*Lucien goes over next to her. She throws herself at him and
begins to slap him and lash out at him with her fists. She's
furious. Lucien in turn loses his temper and begins to hit back,
harder and harder. France tries to protect herself from his blows
with her hands.*

*Some time later the grandmother opens the door silently
and peeks inside. She sees Lucien putting his shirt back on.
France is lying on the bed, almost naked, her face to the wall.
Seeing the old lady, Lucien walks over to the door and closes it in
her face.*

*He pauses a moment by the bed, gazing down at France.
Then from beneath a piece of furniture he takes out his old
cardboard suitcase and starts filling it with his socks and shirts,
which he takes from a closet. He has trouble closing the suitcase.*

*Without looking back at France, he walks out into the
hallway, where he picks up his soap, shaving brush, and razor,
which he slips into his pocket.*

*He plants himself squarely in front of the grandmother
and hands her a wad of money, then turns and leaves.*

39

At the bar of the Grotto Hotel there is considerably less
light than usual. Semidarkness all around the bar. Hippolyte
is behind the bar, while Aubert and Lucien are seated on bar
stools on the other side. The strange lack of light, and the deserted atmosphere, conveys an impression of crepuscular desolation. Aubert is half drunk. He speaks thickly and slowly.

AUBERT: If it hadn't been for that fall, I would have
made the Tour de France for sure. . . . Even a cham-
pion like Bartali never scared me. . . .

Hippolyte is listening carefully, as though he were trying to capture something almost inaudible. Lucien seems bored.

AUBERT: The Italians have always been good bike racers, but they never scared me. . . .

Just then, Faure and two SS arrive, pushing ahead of them a French officer dressed in the uniform of the Free French Forces. The man, who is handcuffed, is trying very hard, under obviously difficult circumstances, to maintain his dignity. He seems contemptuous of his captors.

FRENCH OFFICER (*to the Germans*): And I say to you once again that I'm a French officer. I am fighting for my country. I demand to be treated in accordance with the rules of war. . . .

FAURE: That's right. You tell 'em. . . .

He pushes the officer in the general direction of the staircase.

FRENCH OFFICER (*voice over*): You'd better watch your step. You're soon going to have to account for what you've done!

FAURE: Are you going to shut up?

FRENCH OFFICER: I'm a soldier like you. I demand to be treated like a soldier!

The two Germans take him under the arms and push him up the stairs. The man continues to protest to his captors.

Meanwhile, Aubert is still going on about bicycle racing, as though nothing had happened.

AUBERT: You want to know who would have really made me piss in my pants? The Flemish racers! Now those bastards really knew how to race: (*Pause.*) You ever see Sylvère Maes race?

Lucien seems to be only half-listening.

AUBERT: Don't you see, that fall I had; if you want my opinion, somebody monkeyed with the handlebars. . . .

HIPPOLYTE (*concerned*) : You really think so?

AUBERT: I was winning all the races that year. . . .

HIPPOLYTE (*indignantly*): They were jealous of you, Monsieur Aubert.

Aubert throws out his chest. He looks at Hippolyte with an ecstatic smile.

AUBERT: You have no idea what it is to race. . . . (*Pause.*) When I won the selection-trials race in 'thirty-five, my mother thought I was going to be famous.

Aubert crosses his arms on the bar and buries his head in them, as though he were crying.

HIPPOLYTE (*gently*): Come on, Monsieur Aubert, don't take it so hard!

Aubert doesn't move. Lucien glances at him, almost indifferently.

Hippolyte takes out a record from the shelf behind the bar.

HIPPOLYTE (*to Lucien*): It's his favorite song. . . .

He puts on the record, turns back to Lucien, and puts a finger to his lips. Aubert doesn't move. The record he is playing is Django Reinhardt's "Flower of Boredom." Lucien remains impassive. The music only adds to the feeling of desolation and despair.

From the general direction of the second story, we suddenly hear the screams of the French officer who is being tortured. Aubert lifts his head.

AUBERT (*to Hippolyte*): You want to know something? I'm thirty-six. . . . And if today someone were to ask me to make a choice between women and bicycle racing, I think I'd choose bicycle racing.

As Aubert talks, Hippolyte refills his glass. Aubert, who is leaning on the bar, raises the glass to his lips and takes a sip.

Later that same evening. The lamp on the bar is lighted now. The record player is playing another song. Aubert is still in the same spot, his head buried in his hands. Lucien, also at the bar as before, is still drinking. He yawns noisily. Faure comes back downstairs, accompanied by the two Germans, and enters the bar.

FAURE (*to Lucien*): Go upstairs and keep an eye on him. I'll be in the office with these two gentlemen. . . .

Aubert lifts his head. He looks wearily at Faure.

AUBERT: You mean to say you still have the strength to work?

FAURE (*assertively*): More than ever!

He rejoins the Germans, and all three disappear into the office. Aubert, a dazed expression on his face, leans his head on the palm of his hand. Lucien finishes his drink and gets up.

AUBERT: Hang in there, kid, hang in there. . . .

40

Lucien goes upstairs, and enters the bathroom where the prisoner is. It is clear that the bathroom is used not only for interrogations: a woman's dressing gown is hanging on the wall and there are towels next to the sink. Above the sink is a shelf on which stand an assortment of toothbrushes, glasses, toothpaste, bandages, adhesive tape, and Mercurochrome, as well as lipsticks, cold cream, and other cosmetics, which doubtless once belonged to Betty Beaulieu.

The prisoner is seated in the corner near the bathtub. His clothes have been removed, and he is wearing a striped bathrobe of many colors, the kind one frequently sees at the beach. His hands are behind him, and we can see he has been handcuffed to the radiator. We can also see that he has been subjected to at least the initial phase of torture: his face is bruised and swollen. A man of about forty, he conveys a feeling of energy and strikes one as very probably being a career officer.

When Lucien comes in, the officer looks at him in amazement. Lucien sits down, places his hands flat on the table, and lays his chin on top of them. From that position, he gazes at the prisoner, who meets his eyes without flinching. The exchange of looks lasts for several seconds. Lucien picks up a bottle of cognac from the table and takes a swig.

The prisoner makes an effort to establish contact.

FRENCH OFFICER: How old are you?

Lucien doesn't answer. He gets up and paces around the room.

FRENCH OFFICER: What are you doing here anyway?

Lucien walks all the way around the officer's chair.

LUCIEN: I don't talk to strangers. . . .

Lucien goes over to the sink and fiddles with the various articles and toiletries on the shelf, while the French officer vainly tries to get his attention.

FRENCH OFFICER: So, you're working for the Germans? . . . You, a young Frenchman. . . . Aren't you ashamed? . . .

Again he gets no response, and begins to lose his temper.

> FRENCH OFFICER: Don't try and be smart. You know what they're going to do to you? They're going to take you out and shoot you!

Lucien is playing at opening and closing a lady's compact, which makes an irritating click each time he does it. He looks at the prisoner, who seems encouraged that at last he has caught his attention and tries the friendly route.

> FRENCH OFFICER: You don't look like a gangster to me. (*Persuasively*) Listen, I'm going to give you a chance to save your neck: if you'll remove my handcuffs, I'll take you with me. . . . You understand?

Lucien is now playing with a lipstick tube, twisting the bottom so that the lipstick goes in and out of the tube. Then he takes a roll of adhesive tape.

> FRENCH OFFICER: For God's sake, say something! It's your last chance! . . .

Lucien doesn't let him go on: he has cut off a three- or four-inch piece of adhesive tape, which he pastes over the prisoner's mouth.

> LUCIEN: I told you I don't talk to strangers. . . .

Lucien studies the prisoner, then takes from the shelf above the sink the tube of lipstick, with which he draws a pair of lips on the adhesive tape, holding the prisoner by the chin.

Obviously pleased with the result of his labors, Lucien studies the prisoner's face.

Just then we hear from downstairs the sound of submachine-gun fire. Lucien takes out his pistol and runs over to the window. In the courtyard below he sees two Citroën sedans, the doors of which have been removed. The two sentries guarding the entrance to the hotel have been killed and Lucien sees several members of the Resistance, wearing armbands and carrying submachine guns, racing into the hotel.

Lucien dashes out into the hallway and starts downstairs.

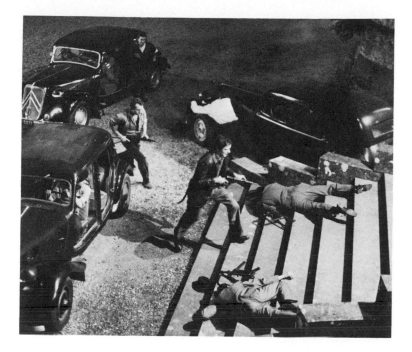

He stops halfway down. On the ground floor the Resistance
fighters are moving into the hotel, firing toward the office where,
Lucien knows, Faure and the two German officers have gone.
Quickly, Lucien runs back upstairs and hides in the room across
the hall from the bathroom, the door to which has remained
open.

Lucien doesn't move a muscle until he hears the two
cars driving away, after which he rushes downstairs.

In the bar all the windows are broken and the floor is
covered with glass. Behind the bar itself most of the bottles are
broken and the mirrors shattered. A great stillness. Aubert is in
the same position as before, that is, with his head buried in his
arms leaning on the bar, but his back is riddled with bullets.
Hippolyte has also been killed and is sprawled behind the bar
with his head cocked crazily to the left. Struck dumb, Lucien
stands there for a long moment. Then he hears a voice calling.

VOICE: Hello! . . . Hello! . . . Kommandantur! . . .
Hello! . . . Hello! . . . Yes. . . . Hello! . . . Hello! . . .
Give me the Kommandantur!

*Lucien enters the office. One of the Germans is dead. Faure, who
has been wounded, is leaning weakly against the table, feverishly
hanging onto the telephone.*

41

Lucien, carrying a submachine gun, gets out of a German
military vehicle and follows a German noncommissioned officer
into Horn's house. Before they go in, we see a group of French
civilians being herded down the street by several German
soldiers.
At the door at the top of the spiral staircase, the German
knocks. France opens the door.

THE GERMAN SOLDIER (*reading a paper*): Mademoiselle
France Horn?

FRANCE: Yes.

The grandmother has materialized behind France.

THE GERMAN SOLDIER (*reading*): Madame Bella Horn?

The old lady does not reply.

The German soldier goes into the room, but Lucien remains behind on the top of the stairs. The German, who speaks
very good French, begins to speak as though reciting a written
order.

THE GERMAN SOLDIER: You can take with you a small
suitcase or knapsack. . . . Only personal effects. . . .
No foodstuffs, no books, no money. . . . You have only
a few minutes. . . .

FRANCE: But. . . .

THE GERMAN SOLDIER (*making an effort to be friendly*):
Hurry up. . . . You're not the only ones who're leaving.

I have a lot of other people on my list. There was, as you may know, a very serious crime committed. . . .

As the German is saying all this, Lucien comes into the room, seemingly awkward and embarrassed, still carrying his gun. France sees him and casts an icy glance in his direction.

A few minutes later. The German soldier is seated, smoking a cigarette. France is helping her grandmother pack a little suitcase. The old lady puts her box of tea, a saucepan, and her deck of cards into the suitcase. France is holding a small leather suitcase. Lucien is pacing back and forth in the room. As he passes a small table, he happens to see the gold pocket watch he gave Horn. He stops, picks it up, and puts it in his pocket. The German soldier, who saw him take it, gets to his feet.

THE GERMAN SOLDIER: Monsieur Lacombe, you are working for the German police. . . . There are no thieves in the German police. . . . Give me what you just took.

Lucien takes the watch from his pocket and, with obvious reluctance, hands it to the German, who smiles at him in a most overbearing way.

42

The German leads the way down the spiral staircase, followed by France, then the grandmother, who is having trouble making it down. Lucien brings up the rear. The old lady stumbles and is helped by France.

Suddenly, without any prior sign or warning, Lucien raises his gun and fires it at the German soldier, who crumples immediately. From this point on, everything happens very fast. Lucien bends over and takes the gold watch from the German's pocket. His eyes meet France's. He goes back up a few steps and takes France by the arm, wanting to spirit her away, but she wrenches free of his grasp.

FRANCE (*indicating her grandmother*): I'm staying with her.

Lucien has a moment's hesitation, then he moves up and takes Madame Horn by the arm and helps her down the stairs by literally carrying her, without sparing her.

43

We next see Lucien, France, and her grandmother in a Citroën sedan. Lucien turns into a narrow, deserted street, which emerges into the countryside. He is driving very fast. France looks at him.

FRANCE: Where are we going?

LUCIEN: I don't know . . . to Spain.

44

The car is stopped along the road, somewhere out in the country. The car is smoking, and Lucien is poking around under the hood, trying to figure out what is wrong. He shakes his head.

45

      Lucien, France, and her grandmother are walking through the woods. The grandmother, who is very slow afoot, is being helped by France. Lucien is walking ahead, the submachine gun in one hand and the luggage in the other. He turns around several times, obviously impatient at the slow progress they're making. Exhausted, the old lady sits down in the grass. Lucien retraces his steps and, with France's help, lifts her to her feet. At the top of a small hill they see through the trees the ruins of a house. The whole place seems completely abandoned.

      Lucien, followed close behind by France and the old lady, goes into the house. In the main room, which is completely dilapidated, are a rickety table, a few wicker chairs, and a fireplace. On the wall is an old calendar dated 1933.

      The grandmother sits down on one of the chairs; she looks as though she couldn't take another step. She has set down her purse on the table in front of her. France also sits down, looking tired and absent, as though her thoughts were elsewhere. She glances over at her grandmother, and sees that she is checking the contents of her purse.

      Lucien leaves the house and takes a walk through the surrounding area, as though reconnoitering. He scans the horizon, the sun-drenched countryside, looks up at the sky, then at the ruins of the house. He goes over to a kind of barn, where he discovers a supply of firewood. He takes several logs under his arms, and rejoins the women in the house. He sets the logs down near the fireplace. The grandmother says something in German. She is still seated in the same chair at the table, counting her cards. Lucien looks over at France.

    LUCIEN: What's she saying?

    FRANCE: One of her cards is missing. . . .

From this point on, there will be no further chronological progression, but a number of long sequences, as though one were patiently following the movements and gestures of the three

people. They will never speak, or only rarely. Nor will there be any further reference to the war: in this sun-drenched setting, with no other human being present, we will have the feeling of being outside of time, outside of history, in a kind of eternity in which the most basic activities of life are repeated endlessly and monotonously over and over again. These final scenes, which are simultaneously sad and serene, will be like a long, sustained organ pedal point.

46

Lucien, alone in the woods. It is early morning. Lucien is setting a primitive trap. Then he walks over to take up a post from where he can keep watch on the trap. He is carrying a beat-up pouch, in which he keeps the game. He waits. He looks in the pouch and takes a dead rabbit from it, then gazes all around at the beauties of nature.

Lucien walks toward the house, carrying his old game pouch.

He goes inside. The grandmother is seated at the table, playing solitaire. France is poking the fire, in preparation for cooking. An old kettle sits next to the fireplace. Savagely, Lucien empties his game pouch: three or four dead rabbits tumble onto the table. France, who has turned around, looks at Lucien with

horror. The grandmother has stopped her game of cards, and she too is looking at the rabbits, her eyes large with wonder.

A lunch. France and her grandmother are seated next to each other. Lucien is opposite them. They are all eating with their hands. With a pocket knife, Lucien cuts up the rabbit and hands various pieces to France and her grandmother. There are no plates, and they all eat directly off the table. In the middle of the table is a kind of nondescript receptacle filled with water, which each drinks from in turn.

47

Lucien and France outside in the woods. Lucien is inspecting one of the traps he has set. They are walking side by side. At one point, Lucien shoots a bird with his slingshot. He takes the tiny body of the bird in his hands and brings it over to France, pretending that he wants to slip it down inside her blouse. She screams and runs away. Lucien runs after her and catches her. They look at each other. France is seated at the base of a tree, still looking at Lucien. She is out of breath. She stretches out full-length and puts her arms behind her head. Lucien is standing two or three yards away. She is looking at Lucien, squinting now because of the sun. He comes over beside her. Timidly, she reaches up and touches him.

48

France and Lucien are walking back to the house. On the threshhold the old lady is standing. We can see her in the distance. She is looking for them.

49

Lucien outside, on a bright, sunny afternoon. He is hiding up in a tree, watching France, who is thirty or so yards away.

FRANCE: Lucien!

France stops and looks around.

FRANCE: Lucien! Lucien!

She seems more and more frightened. From time to time she stops walking, as though discouraged. Then she starts walking again, still calling Lucien. He continues to observe her with a kind of indifference, without climbing down out of the tree.

50

Evening, before the fireplace. The grandmother is playing her game of solitaire. France, who is also seated at the table, is reading a volume of poems her father wrote. Lucien, on the floor in front of the fire, is going through the contents of Horn's suitcase. He takes out a packet of money, then a photograph. He looks at the picture, which is dedicated at the bottom. He gets up and shows the photo to France.

LUCIEN: Who's that?

FRANCE (*glancing at the picture*): Sacha Guitry.

France has gone back to her book. Lucien resumes his position by the fire, and takes several other packets of money from the suitcase, amusing himself by arranging them side by side on the floor. France gets up.

FRANCE: Good night.

THE GRANDMOTHER (*not lifting her eyes*): *Gute Nacht.*

France leaves the room. Lucien remains for a moment next to the fire, then follows France upstairs. The old lady's eyes follow him. At the top of the stairs France is waiting for him with a smile. Then suddenly she disappears into the attic.

In the semidarkness, a strange chase ensues, as France and Lucien play hide-and-seek, running and crawling across the hay. They are overcome with an attack of the giggles. Downstairs the old lady hears them and raises her head.

51

Before dawn Lucien prowls in the vicinity of a farm. He moves toward the main building, goes inside, his game bag over his shoulder.

The room is in semidarkness. On the wall hams are hanging. Quickly, Lucien fills his pouch, then dashes out of the building. Somewhere nearby a dog barks.

52

Lucien is sleeping out of doors. France, carrying a heavy stone, tiptoes toward him. She remains motionless beside him, and for a moment we have the impression she is going to dash the stone down on his face. But she does not; she stands there holding the stone, as though she can't make up her mind.

53

Stretched out in the grass, France is reading a book. Her grandmother is playing her eternal game of solitaire at a nearby table. Beside her, Lucien is cleaning his submachine gun, whose parts he puts on the table as he finishes cleaning them.

54

Outside in the woods, France and Lucien are running. They are out of breath. Laughing.

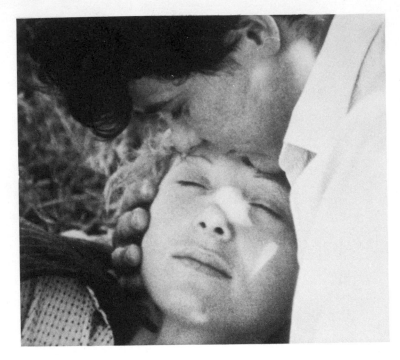

55

France is naked, bathing in a stream. It is another bright, sunny day. A few yards away, Lucien is lying on his back, chewing a piece of hay and watching her. Then he closes his eyes. France stretches and in turn scrutinizes Lucien carefully.

Over Lucien's face appear the following two sentences: "Lucien Lacombe was arrested on October 12, 1944. Tried by a military court of the Resistance, he was sentenced to death and executed."